A NOVEL

the fall

A NOVEL

the fall

KIRSTEN LASINSKI

MOODY PUBLISHERS
CHICAGO

Library of Congress Cataloging-in-Publication Data

Lasinski, Kirsten.
The fall / Kirsten Lasinski.
p. cm.
ISBN 0-8024-1405-2
1. Friendship–Fiction. 2. Sacrifice–Fiction. I. Title.

PS3612.A84F35 2003
813'.54--dc21

2003005727

1 3 5 7 9 10 8 6 4 2

Printed in the United States of America

In dedication to the Redeemer,
who bought me at a price,
and to all those who have loved
and supported me along the way.

"The woman was convinced.
The fruit looked so fresh and delicious,
and it would make her so wise!
So she ate some of the fruit.
She also gave some to her husband,
who was with her. Then he ate it, too.
At that moment, their eyes were opened,
and they suddenly felt shame . . ."
Genesis 3:6–7 (New Living Translation)

Prologue

Where could your father be?" Sandra Jackson peered out the window of the small ground-level apartment at the gathering clouds.

Morris sighed and shifted his weight on the couch. He knew what she was doing. He watched her lean her ribs into the windowsill, her head propped on her hand and her breath clouding the glass. He waved to that same watching silhouette, traced against the faded curtains, each morning as he left for school. She was worrying.

A gust of wind tore a paper from the gutter. Sandra shivered as a streetlight crackled to life against the bruise of the evening sky.

"This snow is really supposed to pick up," she said to no one in particular, letting the curtain flutter back into place. "Up to a foot by morning." A smile eased the line between her brows as she pulled her sweater around her shoulders and

turned to Morris. "That could mean a snow day tomorrow for you, young man."

Morris frowned into the pages of his book. "You really think so?"

"Anything's possible." She leaned over the back of the couch where he lay stretched beneath an afghan.

Morris deliberated for a moment. "If there's a good chance school will be canceled tomorrow"—he paused for effect—"why am I doing this homework?"

Sandra ruffled her son's cropped Afro.

"Nice try," she laughed. "You're doing your homework so you can be prepared for class. My Morris is always prepared."

He cringed and buried his head in the book. That's what you think.

A month had gone by since his teacher first mentioned the new white dress shirts needed for the school pictures tomorrow —a month of weekly reminders and written notices, one of which lay wadded beneath the books in his backpack at that very moment. How could he have forgotten? He knew he couldn't tell his mom at four o'clock on a dark winter evening that he needed a new shirt by the next morning. He would never hear the end of it. So at recess he had dashed across the street to a pay phone at the gas station.

"Dad," he yelled into the receiver, "could you buy me a white shirt on your way home? I need it for class pictures tomorrow."

Saul Jackson's sigh was barely audible above the roaring of the machines. In his mind Morris saw the giant presses of the paper mill grinding out reams of scalding newsprint. He thought about his dad's aching feet and felt a knot cinching in his gut.

"Morris," Saul said, "isn't this something you could ask your mother?"

Morris fidgeted on the sidewalk, grinding the toe of his sneaker into the cement. "I forgot!" he yelled. "I need the shirt for tomorrow, but I forgot until today."

There was a pause.

"Okay. I can pick up a shirt on the way home," Saul yelled. "Just tell your mother I'll be a little late for dinner."

Morris had set the phone in its cradle and walked away, wondering if he should say a prayer for his father's safety. He kicked an empty bottle into the curb and watched with satisfaction as it shattered. He didn't really know how to pray, but he guessed it didn't matter. His mother already spent more than enough time on her knees for all of them.

Morris propped himself up on the couch and watched the snowflakes settle on the withered grass outside. What was taking him so long? Maybe there was a line at the store, a rush of other fathers whose children had also forgotten their shirts.

Sandra went back to the kitchen to spoon the drippings of the pork roast over the potatoes. Morris set his homework aside as she left and turned his attention to a squirrel shaking the branches of the tree outside the window as it scavenged for food. It scurried for cover at the sound of heavy boots on the doorstep.

"Dad's home!" Morris yelled as Saul's bulky frame filled the doorway. Morris threw the afghan aside and lunged for his father, flinging his knobby arms around Saul's middle as he had been doing since he learned to stand. Saul's warm presence, brushed with snow, filled the small room.

"Aren't you eager to see me tonight?" he laughed.

Morris hesitated. Maybe I should ask how his day was. *He pulled away from the soft flannel of Saul's shirt. "What kept you?" he ventured, borrowing his mother's favorite phrase.*

Saul peeled off his coat. "There was a minor emergency at the plant. A machine backfired and stripped some gears. One of my guys almost lost an arm." He rubbed his eyes wearily. "It's a miracle we don't have more injuries there."

"Wow." Morris didn't know what to say. He knew it was bad timing, but he couldn't wait any longer. "Did you get my shirt?"

Saul smacked his forehead with his palm. "Morris, I completely forgot," he confessed. "How important is that shirt?"

Morris thought of his teacher and his eager classmates. He looked at the tired lines around his father's mouth. I can't be the only one to forget.

"It's important," he mumbled.

Saul grabbed a heavier coat off the rack by the door. "I'll go get it right now," he said.

Sandra appeared from the kitchen and sneaked into her husband's arms for a squeeze and a kiss.

"All right, you two, that roast won't wait forever." She waved her wooden spoon for emphasis. "Go wash up so we can eat."

Morris trained his eyes on his feet.

"Actually, Sandy," Saul said, giving her hand a gentle squeeze, "there's one more thing I need to do. I forgot something important at work and need to run back for it."

"But you must be starving," she protested. "Whatever it is, it can't be important enough to send you out into the cold on a night like this."

Saul glanced at his son. "Actually, it is. You and Morris go ahead. I'll just be a few minutes; I promise." He backed toward the door.

"I'll keep your plate warm in the oven, Saul. But please" —Sandra paused at the door to the kitchen—"be careful."

Morris rolled his eyes. Sometimes his mother worried too much.

Saul smiled over them both. "I'll be right back." He pulled on his gloves and ducked out into a world gone suddenly white. Morris shivered at the sight of the falling snow, pumping through a pipeline from heaven to earth. He could hear his mother singing in the kitchen, an old song for no one but herself. The warm smell of home enveloped him as he leaned against the door frame, watching his father stride toward the car through the shining veil of snow.

Chapter 1

It was a gray and threatening Monday afternoon. The sky crouched low over the city's rooftops, muttering of impending rain as it churned against the boxy skyline. The air clung to Morris's neck like a damp dish towel as he propped open the back door of the gymnasium with a rock and stepped into the alley.

The adjoining building belonged to an upscale chiropractor whose misaligned clientele received their adjustments each week with a few swift thumps on the back and cranks of the head. They left the building cracking their necks in a nervous tick and fiddling with their leather-clad phones, and as they drove away in their predictable black BMWs, Morris marveled that anyone would pay to have his spine yanked around like that.

He stifled a shiver and chided himself for leaving his jacket at home. Winter was sluicing its way into spring, and soft spring rains still slicked the city more evenings than not. Hauling three fifty-gallon trash cans to the dumpsters, he emptied them in a fluttering glory of construction paper, candy wrappers, and pencil shavings. A square of paper, stiff with paint, sifted to the top of the rustling pile. It was a portrait of a boy and a smiling dog beneath a rainbow, lovingly slathered in one of the art classes. Morris smiled at the thought of the happy artist, frolicking in the grass with his pet. *What a wonderful world.*

Thunder rolled over in the distance, and the sky began to drain. Just then, a patient stepped out the side door of the doctor's office and into the alley, jingling his keys at his side. His shirt was untucked, and his graying hair stuck out in wings from the sides of his head.

Morris slung the trash cans over his shoulder and started for the school. The patient whirled around at the unexpected sound, let out what Morris thought was a rather feminine shriek, clawed open the door to the office, and dived back inside. Morris stopped in his tracks. Realizing what an imposing figure he must have made, looming massive in the shadows behind the frightened executive, he rolled his eyes as he backed into the school.

"All right," he yelled. "I'm going inside now. It's safe to come out, little businessman." It was mean, but he couldn't resist. "The scary black man is gone." He pulled the door shut and slid the bolt into place with a satisfying click. Wars were undoubtedly raging somewhere in the world, but for the moment all was right with one small corner of it.

In the hallway, he wrung a mop into a bucket of disinfectant and slapped it against the floor with a wet *thwack.* Bubbles scattered weakly on the murky tile, while outside rain flowed in sheets down the windows that ringed the front of

Quiley Heights Elementary School. Morris fell into the rhythm of his work, lulled by the drumming of the rain.

Thunder cracked overhead. Lightning flickered over a tree across the street, pausing for an instant to dart its searing tongue among the branches as a painful creaking rent the air, and the stalwart oak trembled and split. The largest branch snapped from the trunk and crashed into the house below, sending a quarter of the black-shingled roof shivering to the ground. The light withdrew, and the sky seemed darker than before. Sirens whirred toward the house as neighbors clotted in the street. *Good old Quiley Heights. There's always a cop around when you need one.*

Quiley Heights was a sprawling urban village of sorts. A poor neighborhood, but not the poorest in the city, it was the kind of place where children played in vacant lots shadowed by nightclubs and parking garages and grew to love the color gray. Where a woman could still walk the streets at night if she kept one eye over her shoulder and both hands clutching her purse. Where elderly widows crowded into church basements for weekly bingo games, knitted sweaters for the Salvation Army, and churned out casseroles and pies with surprising alacrity at the slightest whiff of tragedy. Morris still had a tuna surprise stashed in his freezer from the time his cat ran away.

He quickly mopped the last stretch of hallway, smiling ruefully at the thought of hundreds of little boots tracking mud onto his pristine floors the next day. These same little people clogged the toilets, threw up in the cafeteria, and filled the trash cans to overflowing, but he wouldn't have missed them for the world. When it came to children, the way he figured, the mess was part of the joy.

He wrestled the mop and bucket into the supply closet with a grimace. What was that odor? Was one of the kids growing a science experiment in a corner somewhere? He was hurrying through his chores, checking his supply of Windex with a practiced eye, when a sweet smell wafted into the cramped space.

"Hi, Morris."

His scalp grew disturbingly warm at the sound of her voice. He stepped into the hall and slammed the door behind him, praying that he had sufficiently trapped the awful stench.

"Hi, Sheri." He couldn't help but smile as he said her name. *I must look like an idiot, standing here with this huge grin.* He cleared his throat. "What are you doing here so late?"

Sheri Wallace taught the first grade at Quiley Heights with all the idealism and energy of her twenty-five years. It wasn't unusual for her to stay late into the night turning her classroom into a South American jungle or an Egyptian archaeological dig. Morris had caught her on more than one occasion with scraps of construction paper clinging to her clothes and smudges of paint on her fingers. But even the occasional wearing of school supplies couldn't detract from her loveliness. She was slightly taller than average, slender, and pretty enough to unnerve him, with wavy hair to her collarbone and wide, dark eyes.

"I had spelling tests to grade." She shifted an armload of books to her hip. A spiral of silky hair dropped over her forehead, and he clenched his fingers at his side, fighting the urge to tuck it behind her ear.

"Mmm-hmm." He nodded sympathetically. "At least you didn't have to clean the boys' bathroom." She laughed, and he marveled at her perfect teeth.

"So," she said casually, "Hattie's birthday is next week. I think we should throw her a surprise party. The kids would love it."

He gaped. "How did you find that out? I've been trying to weasel Hattie's birthday out of her for years."

Sheri smiled sheepishly. "While I was in Vern's office yesterday, I noticed that the new receptionist was updating the personnel files. To make a long story short . . ."

"You peeked!" He laughed as she squirmed.

"I know that's terrible," she sighed, "but I was dying of curiosity."

Morris glanced over his shoulder and lowered his voice. "Did you happen to see how old she is?"

Sheri opened her large eyes even wider. "Are you crazy? That's like asking me what kind of underwear the pope wears."

He snickered. "We'll throw her the perfect party. She'll never speak to us again, but it'll be worth it."

"I'll handle the decorations," Sheri said.

He couldn't resist. "Looks like you've been decorating tonight," he said, as he gently tugged a length of silver streamer from her hair.

"Tomorrow we're starting our unit on the solar system. I was trying to make that ugly room look a little more like outer space . . ." She trailed off, waving a graceful hand at her classroom across the hall.

"You've already got one heavenly body," Morris said, then chomped down on his tongue, hoping to bite it in two. Why did he always turn into a blathering Neanderthal around her?

Sheri laughed, and he sighed inwardly with relief. Thank goodness the girl had a sense of humor.

"Come take a look and tell me what you think."

The room was hushed and dim as they entered. He puzzled at the cool breeze that pressed against his face. Where was that coming from? There were no windows in Sheri's classroom.

She flipped a switch. "Let there be light," she said.

"Ahhhh." Tiny white bulbs scattered across the ceiling cast a soft glow. Cloudlike wisps of tulle hovered gently below the lights, riding the invisible currents of the air, and the familiar desks and chairs gleamed like components of a space station in the cold, pure radiance.

"Welcome to the Milky Way," she said. The dingy walls of the classroom had disappeared, covered over in ripples and folds of thick velvet the color of the midnight sky.

Morris turned to face her, words crowding his throat. He wanted to tell her how much he admired her resourcefulness, her enthusiasm for every little thing in life. It was why he liked her . . . why he loved her. *Loved her?* He froze. *Do I love her?* She was waiting for him to speak, the stars reflected in her eyes. He panicked.

"Where's the sun?" he blurted. *Real smooth, Morris.*

She reached around him to flip a switch on the wall and split the room with a bright band of golden light. A half-sphere of yellow glass softened the intensity of the naked bulb that was anchored to the ceiling near the door.

"It's beautiful," he said, "but isn't that the lightbulb from the exit sign?"

"Yes, and that's one of Miss Hattie's mixing bowls," she laughed. "But don't tell the kids." The spell was broken. "Let me turn off the solar winds, and we can get out of here." She clicked off a fan hidden on the floor and scooped up her pile of papers.

He took the stack of books from her and opened the door.

"Allow me to walk you to your car, Miss Wallace."

She smiled up at him, and there was something in the curve of her lips he couldn't quite read. "You're always a gentleman, Morris."

"That's what my mother raised me to be." He wiggled his eyebrows wickedly, grabbed an umbrella from the lost and found, and escorted her to the parking lot.

❖ ❖ ❖

Morris usually timed his dinners by the pounding cycles of the commuter trains that ran by his apartment. It took four trains to bake a potato, three to cook a meat loaf to moist perfection, and two for macaroni and cheese. Some would have considered the incessant grinding of the trains a nuisance, but he found them soothing. In a strange way they kept him from feeling alone. That night, however, he lost track of the trains.

His fingers traced mindless patterns on the lumpy arm of his favorite chair as he mulled over his conversation with Sheri that afternoon. Visions of her clogged his brain: beautiful Sheri waiting for him at the altar in a trailing white dress, Sheri with wailing bundles in her arms, Sheri growing old and fat and gray? He grimaced.

I can't think about this anymore. He picked up the paper from the floor. *Let's see. The mayoral election is coming up soon, isn't it?* He skimmed the day's headlines and forced his mind to other thoughts.

Flipping through the travel section, he wondered how much it would cost to fly first-class to Nassau. *More than I'll ever have.* He turned the page. A strip of glittering sand melted at the prodding of the ocean's waves. What was it about those pictures? The landscape seemed so familiar. In an uninvited burst of memory, bright snapshots of a dream from the night before shuffled through his mind. The seamless bellies of birds against a deep blue sky, the smell of a humid greenhouse, cool water under his tongue. How odd that he could have forgotten such a vivid dream. He folded the paper with an inward sigh.

Is something burning?

The smell of burned cheddar wafted into the living room, and Morris's nostrils stiffened as he remembered the macaroni. He snapped from his reverie, leaped up from an old chair that leaked stuffing at the seams, cursed, and waved a battered pot holder to disperse the smoky air. The ancient smoke detector in the hall gave a piercing warble and died.

He hung the pot holder, crocheted for him by his landlady, on a nail above the stove and scraped the charred layer of cheese from his meal with a fork, longing briefly for a frozen TV dinner. The desire quickly passed. Nothing in his kitchen came from a box, not even the simplest of comfort foods, and he would have gone hungry before he lowered himself to eating anything involving powdered cheese.

He salvaged what he could of the macaroni and cheese and fought a stab of remorse as he chewed. Good cooking reminded him of his mother. *I should call her. It's been almost two weeks since we talked.* The food solidified to a block in his stomach. *Maybe tomorrow.*

He washed the dishes and set them to dry in a rack by the sink, bolted the flimsy front door, wondered if the drunk he had given pocket money to that afternoon was actually going to buy food with it, and walked the short hall to the bathroom. It was early yet, but he would be up with the rising of the sun to catch the train to work.

Thoughts of the kids at school chased through his mind as he brushed his teeth. Little Connor Parker was having a hard time with his parents' divorce, which explained his recent behavior, including the glue incident in Sheri's class. His mother had come to pick him up from school the week before, hiding behind dark sunglasses and a cloud of sprayed blonde hair.

She picked at her plastic nails, pursed her overly red lips at Sheri, and told her to call if Connor had any problems.

"But don't ever call his father," she had said while Connor writhed at the end of her hand like a trout hooked through the lip. "He doesn't care."

Morris hoped to have children of his own someday, but that seemed like a distant dream. He couldn't even keep a girlfriend for more than a couple of months, despite his broad shoulders and frank, smiling eyes. Most women his age found his stability and quiet depth boring, and because there were plenty of richer, flashier men around, they came and went from his life without leaving any real scars on his satisfied heart. Overall, he was a contented young man.

He snipped off a length of dental floss and wound it carefully around his thumbs. He had no debts, paid his bills on time, helped his landlady take out her trash, and kept his apartment clean. He had a job he found fulfilling, and he was making—at least he hoped he was making—a difference in hundreds of little lives. He scrutinized his reflection in the mirror. Suddenly he saw himself, trembling and bent with age, smiling as he climbed to the podium to receive the award. He straightened his tie with arthritic fingers and choked back a flood of emotion. Thousands of former students cheered as he began his speech in a voice quavering with gratitude.

Grow up. He pinched the bath mat between his toes. *They don't give the Nobel prize to janitors.*

Even so, he was happy with the world he had built for himself. He dropped the floss into the trash and noticed how quiet his small apartment had become. The trains had purged themselves of passengers and stopped their routes for the night, and his fractious neighbors for once weren't arguing. In the sudden stillness he felt strangely lonely, and a nagging suspicion fluttered at the back of his brain. It was ridiculous. *There's nothing missing. What could be missing? Except maybe a trip to the Bahamas.*

He quit his musing, turned off the light, and went to bed.

Chapter 2

Morris woke up slowly, sensing rather than seeing a light through his eyelids. He cracked his left eye open, squinting hard with his right, and groaned. *Is that the sun?* Waves of suffocating sleep pinned him to the bed as he struggled to surface.

He focused on a cluster of leaves several feet above his head. *Leaves?* They fluttered in the breeze, tapping with the sound of hushed applause. *Leaves.* He rolled with difficulty onto an elbow and looked around, surprised to find himself stretched in the shade of a short, far-reaching tree. *Where am I?*

As a child he had sometimes roamed the house in his sleep, waking up curled beneath a pile of clothes in the laundry room or sitting at the kitchen table with a spoon in his hand, but he had never ventured outdoors.

There aren't any trees in my neighborhood. He pulled himself up, unsure of whether to be frightened or glad, and looked around.

Branches twisted horizontally from the squat trunk, spreading a wide canopy of shade, while leaves arched their waxy backs to the sun. The ground was covered in a softer, slicker version of grass than that which grew in Quiley Heights, piled beneath his frame in a soft, fragrant bed. Clouds hovered in creamy clumps on the horizon of a vivid blue sky. He blinked. *I'm dreaming.*

Three birds flashed across the sky in a staggered line. Two more sailed in from the opposite direction and slid into formation as the group climbed out of sight, then plummeted toward the earth again, wheeling tightly as they dived.

Morris staggered to his feet, rubbing his eyes as a cool breeze rose from the meadows below. In an instant he was blessedly alert, tingling with a pleasant cold as the paralyzing haze slipped from his mind. He laughed and clapped his hands.

Halfway down the hill a stream slipped through the grass, glassy water gushing over rocks yet to be worn smooth. Sand rolled beneath the current, grinding shards of rock and dark mineral deposits into the powdery bed. As Morris watched, a length of silver sliced through the water, then launched itself into the air, spraying an arc of icy droplets into the grass. The fish landed without a splash and darted out of sight.

Morris leaned back and curled the grass between his bare brown toes. Below him the stream tumbled into a meadow of looping grasses and wildflowers, narrowing into coils of gleaming light. Trees dotted the landscape in shady groupings, and hedges of lilacs and wild roses snaked through the grass. In the distance a stretch of low mountains formed a knobby spine against the sky, and a warm breeze wafted from over the hill behind him, carrying the breath of sweet, ripe things.

Tall ferns and tufted fronds of wheat parted easily before him as he drifted through the grass. His outstretched palms brushed the tops of the wild wheat, releasing a wholesome scent from the depths of the ruffled sheaths. He swung his strong, light limbs and climbed the plunging hill, grasping a handful of the slippery grass at the top to pull himself over the edge of the huge plateau.

There he tottered for a moment, the air rushing from his lungs as he stumbled into paradise. *Am I still dreaming? Am I dead?* Countless trees rose up to filter the sunlight, every branch bursting with flowers and fruit. Milky blossoms drifted to the ground and piled up like mounds of spotless snow. Golden nectar streamed down the trunks, painting them with a thin lacquer of light and spicing the air, while heavy fruits snapped from their stems and fell to the cushion of grass all around, splitting open with juicy thumps. Hidden birds sang unending throaty songs.

How long have I been standing here? Hours? Years? A sweet sense of belonging drew Morris in as he realized the truth: His whole life had been nothing more than a tepid dream. He was waking to reality for the first time.

"If I'm dead, I don't want to know," he whispered. The breeze blew and the trees danced, creaking with an audible delight. He ducked beneath the canopy of branches.

A scant thirty feet away, tigers blurred together in rings of orange and black, one heap of rumbling muscle and fur. Morris had seen live tigers only once, on a field trip to the zoo with his second grade class. The irascible cats had slunk back and forth behind the bars, tails lashing the stale air. Now he stood, mouth agape, longing to run his fingers through the plush collars at their necks and feel the power of their paws.

He inched forward, wishing for a concrete moat. When he was twenty feet away, the tigers froze, rolling off of one another as they lifted their nostrils to test the air. He could almost read their thoughts as they eyed him: *New scent, fresh meat, smells juicy.*

The thought occurred to him too late: *Perhaps this isn't the brightest thing I could do.* Morris coiled his legs to leap into the branches of the tree beside him and waited for the claws to fly.

Suddenly a tiny fawn hopped out of the underbrush and into the pile of cats. Morris turned away. He couldn't bear to watch the gentle eyes and soft, spotted hide of the deer shredded into a pile of blood and bones. The largest of the tigers unwound from the rest, slunk several paces deeper into the shade and flopped down with a contented rumble. The fawn sprung over, its spindly legs barely skimming the grass, and curled into a ball against the tiger's heaving side. They were fast asleep before Morris could close his gaping mouth. He willed his eyes to blink. *What is this place?*

In the lush fields beyond the trees, horses galloped in lazy rings, their hooves kneading the earth into clouds of dust. Sunlight flashed on their haunches, while silky tails floated behind, snapping like flags in the breeze.

Morris felt a whisper at his neck. A butterfly perched on his shoulder, awash with the radiant glow of sunlight on its golden wings. The slender body bowed as he brought his arm across his torso and held his first two fingers near the sticky feet. The shadows receded in the growing light of the gilded wings as the butterfly stretched one thin, black leg toward his hand. He bit his lip as the golden sails flapped once, then twice, and the first foot grazed his nail with a touch too light to feel.

The lights went out. Morris froze in the sudden, impenetrable darkness. *What did I do?* Then out of the depths, a bright form bounded his way. It was Sheri, leading her class outside on a summer day. Green fields sprang up under their feet as they ran, and a blazing sun unfurled in the sky. The children skipped past him, tumbling in the grass as they slipped into the darkness again, and another image appeared.

His mother stood humming in the kitchen. She pulled a warm loaf of bread out of the oven and set a buttered slice on the table for him beside a cold glass of milk. The bright colors of her apron melted into black as she reached out to ruffle his hair, and another light, brighter than the rest, bled into the darkness.

Saul pulled him into a hug. *Dad?* Warm flannel brushed his cheek and the strong, steady thump of a living heart beat a pattern in his ears. He buried his face in Saul's neck, laughing as the arms squeezed tighter. *Dad?* The darkness receded. *Don't go.*

The light returned. Through the empty circle of his arms, he saw the fields shimmering in the heat. The butterfly turned away, circling him twice before lifting above the roof of the trees. The shadows engulfed him again, and he stepped with a shiver into the sun. *Forget it.*

He pushed his thoughts of Saul away, letting the memory of his father's arms evaporate in the bright light of day. *Just enjoy this.* The sun warmed the planes of his cold face and streaked along the rims of his eyes until his eyelids burned. His cheeks flushed with an unexpected heat, and the sunlight nipped at his forehead. He pried his eyes open. It seemed to be growing brighter. *It can't be.* Tears streamed down his cheeks, but he couldn't look away. A sound, a siren blared from the center of the flaring sun, growing louder and shriller as the light increased. *Stop it.* He flailed helplessly at the burning brightness. *Stop it.* He slapped wildly at the piercing scream. Something bashed against his head.

In an instant he was awake. The sheets were twisted tightly around his waist, and his battered alarm clock lay in his lap. *Ouch.* He rubbed the growing lump on his head. His ears sang as he staggered across the room and pulled back the curtains. The wilting half-light of the dirty city dawn crept into his room. Somewhere below, tires screeched in protest as a driver stomped on the brakes. A sickly attempt at a rosy blush died in the sky. *Welcome back.* He shuffled down the hall and stubbed his toe on the bathroom door with a loud curse.

As he leaned his face against the cold tiles of the shower and let the steaming water pound at the knots in his neck, only one thing was clear. He had to stop having those dreams.

Chapter 3

The stainless steel doors slid open with a sterile puff of air. Harried commuters rushed from the train and stumbled toward the light of day as a garbled voice announced times and destinations over the departing crush. Morris loped through the station, wondering briefly about the vague creature behind that voice. He could almost see her: pale as a mist, bloodshot eyes fixed upon that great, unblinking clock every moment of every day as she sat bouncing one crossed leg over the other in a dim booth beneath the street. No wonder she mumbled.

The waiting crowd stamped their feet in the cool of the hollowed underground and pushed forward onto the narrow train, pawing at one another for a chance to squeeze into the humming chute that would shuttle them away. He hunkered down at the back of the line but didn't go unnoticed for long.

The questions, familiar to him as his own name, started with a curious construction worker beside him.

"Hey," the man said, tipping his hard hat back for a better look, "you look familiar. Do you play football?"

Morris shook his head.

"Basketball?"

"Only for fun," he answered, "not professionally."

A squat woman swathed in plaid chimed in from the other side. "Really?" she screeched. "You should. You should play football. You could make a lot of money."

It's too early for this.

"Well," he answered slowly, "there are more important things in life than money, aren't there?"

The woman shook her round head until the curls heaped on top trembled with alarm. "You could buy your mama a nice house if you played football," she continued. "I wish my son were your size. I'd make him play football."

Now how am I supposed to respond to that? Give her my condolences on having a shrimpy son?

"I already have a job." He regretted the words even as they left his mouth.

Too late. The woman pounced. "What do you do?"

"I'm a janitor."

She gasped as if he had revealed a fungus between his toes. "Oooooh! A fine figure of a boy like you, a janitor? How do you expect to support your mama on a janitor's salary?"

The construction worker laughed from beneath his hat.

"My mother is taken care of," Morris said firmly. He pointed toward the front of the line. "Look, the line's moving."

The woman whirled around and plunged into the fray, scrapping for a seat near the doors, and Morris slid in behind her, swallowing the urge to tell her that she would make a decent linebacker herself.

No one was moving fast enough. Morris struggled to quell a rising claustrophobia as people pressed against him. He tapped his hand against his leg and thought of wide open spaces. Accusing glares withered an old man who dared to pause at the entrance, then shuffled to the back of the car, clinging to the railings all the way.

Someone behind Morris snorted in frustration. "Hurry up, old man."

"It's not his fault you're late for work," Morris answered, just above the rustle of the crowd. The snorting stopped. He could feel the perpetrator's irritated eyes boring into the back of his head.

What's my problem today? He wasn't the kind of guy to incite a riot on the subway platform. It was odd; he just felt like picking a fight. Wasn't he satisfied with his life? The last thing he had needed was some fantastical dream to point out all the shortcomings of his carefully orchestrated world.

A woman in a business suit and heels teetered by, clutching an overstuffed briefcase and scalding coffee in a flimsy cardboard cup. Morris felt a nudge in his ribs.

"That's a lawsuit waiting to happen." A short, balding man next to him laughed. He looked like a seal tucked into a sleek gray suit. "I should know. I'm a lawyer."

That's nice. I'm a janitor. Morris nodded politely and climbed onto the train before his chatty neighbor could launch into the details of his practice and his chances of making partner. All around him people scrambled for seats. *Poor fools.* They tried to look so nonchalant as they elbowed their way through the crowd.

A stout businessman panted into his cell phone several

seats away. He plopped his bulging attaché on the seat beside him as a woman jiggling a baby on her hip approached. Morris watched with rising irritation as the man turned his back to her and kept yakking. He caught the woman's bewildered gaze and rose to offer his seat. She slid into his place and squeezed his hand. "Thank you," she whispered. The baby batted joyously at the air and drooled on his sleeve.

Morris winked and moved through the crowd to where the sweating executive lolled limply over the seats. In one smooth motion Morris scooped up the offending bag, dropped it neatly at its owner's feet, and settled his large frame into the vacant space, scooting as close to his seatmate as possible. The man gave an indignant start and turned to argue but stalled at the young man's gaze.

"Excuse me," Morris said in a tone that killed the argument before it started.

He relaxed and took in the familiar scene. Young punks in undershirts flexed their tattooed biceps and fiddled with the metal bars screwed into their fleshy faces. Across the car, a man pleaded his case to a woman until permission was given and a phone number was obtained and both parties were left to bask in the glow of their attractive wiles. A clot of hungry college students spread textbooks across their laps for a frantic review before class.

A skimpily dressed, gum-smacking girl who looked too young to legitimately call herself a teenager batted heavily lined eyes at him from across the aisle. Her brief tank top read "Diva" in tarnished rhinestones. What mother would let a girl out of the house like that? Did she even have a mother?

Morris folded his long legs beneath the seat and sighed. Next to the diva a happily preoccupied Asian man with gleaming black hair and a contented smile held a book in his lap. It was small and well worn, the dark leather cracking along the binding and a raggedy tail of ribbon marking his place. As he shifted in his seat the book reared up for a moment, and Morris caught a glint of gold. *Holy Bible.* He groaned inwardly. *Not today. Morris, you picked the wrong seat.*

The myriad street preachers who crowded the city already supplied him with several sermons a week on the evils of money, dancing, gambling, and fun in general as they waved their tattered hats for donations and proclaimed right from wrong for anyone with "ears to hear." Morris gave the Bible-toter one last glance, closed his eyes, and waited for the tirade to begin. Minutes passed. The man didn't stand, clear his throat, or smile broadly at his captive audience. He didn't pull a crumpled hat from his pocket or pass a cup around as an offering plate.

Against all reason, the preacher seemed deeply absorbed in whatever he was reading, with no intention of preaching to anyone. He even managed to tune out the gum cracker to his right and the old woman systematically clearing her throat to his left. *That's new. Someone reading the Bible for pleasure. I guess it takes all kinds.* There was something about the smile hovering on his lips that grated inexplicably on Morris's nerves. Why should that guy be happier than anyone else on the train?

As Morris watched the man across the aisle, a memory crept unbidden to his mind.

❖ ❖ ❖

He was waist high to the world and still clung to his mother's hand as they darted together across the street. His Sunday coat and tie pinched unbearably, and he wondered as he trotted along why God had any interest in what he wore. The white church building towered over them. Morris clambered up the stairs behind his mother and slipped inside, softening in the clutches of the crawling humidity like wax before a flame. It was twenty minutes until the service started, but already the church was thick with rubbing bodies. Why would anyone want to get to church early? Maybe God punished people for being late. From the scraps of sermons Morris caught each week, he gathered that God was a wrathful creature.

They waded through the crowded halls toward the sanctuary, stopping frequently to chat with people. He wiggled impatiently at each stop, wretched and moist and bored by the unchanging vista of belted midriffs and polished shoes and ankles wrapped in hose. His mother's fingers grew slippery, and he let go, careful to keep an eye on her cream-colored pumps. If he lost her in that crowd, he might never find her again.

Inside the sanctuary, hundreds of people crammed together on the rows of wooden pews that splayed out from the elevated stage. The soft fibers of the matching blue velvet carpet and cushions glittered under beaming can lights nestled high in the ceiling. Purple banners with gold braid trim and Bible verses in gold lettering hung limply on the walls, proclaiming the majesty of God to all that entered. A roughly hewn table waited against the back wall of the stage, covered with the finest purple linen and set with a silver challis.

The din grew to a roar as chattering latecomers wedged themselves into the groaning church. Paper fans beat the air into sickly currents around the giant room. The sanctuary was a field of flowered hats and jacketed shoulders. Morris wondered if the women planned to ride to heaven on their hats. There were enough silk flowers and pins and bows to save the whole congregation from the nipping fires of hell, if that were the case.

He coughed as a woman stepped past him in a cloud of perfume. She slid gracefully down the aisle, her shoulders square and her spine a perfect line to her hips. Behind him, an old woman clicked her tongue.

"Janetta Jones shouldn't hold her head so high," she said to the woman beside her. "I heard that Mr. Jones threatened to walk out on her if she didn't learn to cook." Her friend "mmm-hmmed" and nodded in agreement.

"I heard," she added in a reaching whisper, "that she used cinnamon in his eggs one morning when she ran out of paprika." This set the women cackling, to the delight of their curious neighbors. The tale was too good not to be repeated, and soon the whole row was laughing at Mrs. Jones's expense.

Morris felt sorry for the young woman, who looked so beautiful and sad.

His mother halted at their usual spot: the fifth row from the platform. "Close enough," she always said, "but not too close." Sandra Jackson was a big believer in moderation in all facets of life, save church attendance and cooking.

They reached their seats just as an elderly woman perched at the organ began to thump the wheezing pedals. The ancient juggernaut piped, and the choir stood as the singing began. Bodies swayed, robes fluttered, voices thundered and shrilled, and every hand clapped in crisp unison. The singing continued for what seemed an eternity, and Morris began to wonder if that was what heaven would be like. He guessed that would be all right, as long as he was seated near his mom. He could listen to her sing forever, nestled in the soothing warmth of her rich, smooth voice. The men at church seemed to enjoy her voice especially, and sometimes Morris wished his father would come with them.

The choir leader finally sat down, and the tall young

pastor ran down the center aisle and sprang easily up the stairs to the platform. He stopped behind the pulpit, gripped the sides for support, and smiled meaningfully at his new bride of three months in the first row, who blushed meaningfully in response. It was scandalous how loving they were, and some of the lonelier old ladies in the congregation raced home that afternoon to search the Holy Book for any hint of a rebuke against public demonstrations of affection. Perspiration shone on his forehead as he let out a gut-wrenching sigh, then bowed for a moment of silent prayer.

"Brothers and sisters," he began in a voice smooth from rehearsal, "why are we here today?"

Someone coughed at the back of the sanctuary. A baby whimpered in the silence. No one answered. Morris wondered why the preacher was always asking questions that no one answered.

"For what purpose have we gathered here?" he continued. "To sing, to fellowship . . . or to let God search our souls?" His voice fell and his head came up, his eyes smoldering like bits of burning coal under the glorious lights. Then he spoke the words Morris dreaded most as he lowered his head. "Let us pray."

Morris buttoned his eyes obediently. He struggled to stay awake, fighting the draw of the melodic voice, but it was a losing battle. His small brown head nodded to his chest, and whether he slept for minutes or hours he couldn't tell.

A great roar jerked him from blissful oblivion. Was it the end of the world? Was it Armageddon? His eyes snapped open, and he half expected the church to be burning as fire rained from heaven. The pastor was yelling. He tilted the pulpit forward, sweeping the congregation with his piercing eyes as his voice thundered from the stage.

"Do not think, brothers and sisters, that you can run from God! Do not attempt to hide from His ever present eyes!"

Women dabbed their faces with twisted handkerchiefs. Men yanked miserably at their ties.

"For we are all sinners!" He slammed the pulpit with his open palm as he steamed to a climax. "We have eaten the forbidden fruit," he yelled, "and God has seen our sin!"

Morris stiffened in horror and nearly slid from the pew. How did the preacher know? Had God told him? He squirmed in his seat at the memory. The shiny copper bowl of fragrant pears rested on the kitchen counter just within his reach. Mother had told him not to touch them. She needed them for a special recipe. But if she didn't want him to eat them, why did she leave them there? Was she trying to torment him? Maybe if he just touched them, it would be enough. Maybe if he just smelled them, he would be satisfied.

With a furtive glance at the door, he had pulled the bowl onto his lap. The fruit gave easily in his fingers, releasing a spicy odor at his touch. The round bottoms of the pears fit snuggly against his palms and cooled his fevered hands. It was too much to resist. He tore into the fragile skin, slurped at the sweet flesh as the juice streamed down his guilty chin, and gulped his way through two of the untouchable fruits before his hunger subsided. Running from the kitchen, he felt suddenly sick at what he had done.

And now God knew, and the preacher knew, and they were shaming him before the whole church. He was too frightened to look up. He couldn't meet the hundreds of scowling eyes and pointing fingers. As the sermon rolled on above his head, he wriggled away from his mother, tucked his chin deep into his collar, and tried with all his small strength to disappear.

❖ ❖ ❖

The train lurched around a corner, jerking Morris back to the present as it rocked on its wheels. Too late, he realized that the preacher across the aisle was watching his watcher with interest. He smiled as Morris dropped his eyes and awkwardly cleared his throat. There was a faint but unmistakable chuckle from the other side.

The train ground to a halt at its next stop. The man closed his Bible, smiled at Morris, and wove through the crowd toward the exit. Morris followed his dark head through the door with relief. He took a deep breath and tried to put the embarrassing incident from his mind as the Quiley Heights station rolled into view.

The clouds pulled back from the morning sky as the sun bounced into the train with the promise of spring, and Morris felt his mind begin to clear. Another day with one of the most beautiful teachers and some of the best kids in the world couldn't be all that bad. The train ducked beneath the street and squealed in the darkness. The crowd murmured to life as people hustled their stiff limbs toward the exit. Morris hefted his bag to his shoulder and walked off toward the school.

Chapter 4

Quiley Heights Elementary School squatted neatly on its huge, and thankfully flat, blacktop square at the top of the hill, just as it had the night before. From there he could look down over the city and see his mother's apartment building nestled among a cluster of high-rises several miles away. She had sold their tiny house on Chase Street, packed away a lifetime of memories in careful tissue and intermittent tears, and moved into a beautiful new apartment four years ago when she married William.

It had been a lovely wedding. Like any good son Morris just wanted his mother to be happy. He had walked her down the aisle and passed her trembling hand to William that day, glad that she had found a way to leave the past behind. Now he looked down on her apartment and wondered what she was doing. Having breakfast? Making plans for the day with William? He turned back to the school.

The eastern windows, newly washed by the evening rain, were blinding in the rising sun. It was only seven o'clock, still half an hour before school started, and no kids had arrived yet.

He savored the shrill squeak of his shoes on the spotless floors as he strode the shining hallways to the teachers' lounge, where some of the city's finest educators sat huddled around a box of doughnuts, sipping bitter coffee flecked with grounds out of chipped ceramic mugs. The school couldn't afford much more than a closet for the staff room, but Morris took comfort in keeping it clean for his colleagues. He was halfway through the door when a familiar voice rang out.

"Morris! Come here, sugar. Let me look at you."

Miss Hattie Graeble was a plump, matronly masterpiece. She was an institution at Quiley Heights, having seen twenty-two classes of third graders march proudly, under her careful tutelage, into the fourth grade. More importantly, she was a dear friend who always knew what needed to be said and said it.

Morris smiled at her sorry attempt to sound stern, and dimples softened his angular face. Hattie was rarely angry and won over her unruliest students with warmth and persistence. They eventually learned to love and respect her, and more importantly, mind her, and it wasn't unusual for her former students to return for brief visits in her sunny classroom during breaks in their hectic schedules. They grew up into lawyers and dentists and stockbrokers and football players, all attributing their success to a certain third grade teacher who cared enough to pester them into submission and proper spelling. She remembered every one of them by name, peering through the added years and inches to look upon the child she once knew.

Morris knew that Sheri watched this parade from a distance with a sigh of admiration, hoping that someday it might be her students taking a break from their successful lives to pay her visits. It was every teacher's dream to leave such a legacy, he supposed. *Who am I kidding? It's my dream too.*

Hattie perched on the arm of a beaten-down sofa with her perpetual maple bar and diet Coke. She handed him a glazed doughnut on a napkin and squeezed his bicep. She shook her head solemnly, like a doctor relaying awful news. "You're positively wasting away."

He couldn't help but laugh. "Hattie! I weigh over two hundred pounds!"

It had taken two years of her constant badgering to persuade him to call her by her first name, and it still felt awkward on his tongue. She just wasn't the kind of woman you addressed without a title, and Morris, being schooled from birth in proper reverence for one's elders, had a hard time getting past it.

"Yes, but you're so tall," she persisted. "You need more meat to cover those long bones."

He obligingly munched at his doughnut and scanned the room. The teachers were huddled in chatting clumps around the watercooler and the sink or in the corners posing serious concerns to one another. Sheri was scrounging gracefully in the fridge for a soda. Everything she did was graceful. She probably picked her nose gracefully, he thought.

Hattie's voice broke into his reverie. "What are you doing Saturday night?" she asked a little too casually.

He knew that voice, that forced nonchalance. He backed away from the couch. "No way, Hattie!" He couldn't be firm enough. "I'm not letting you set me up again."

"But, Morris," she pleaded, "this girl is lovely. She's my hairdresser's niece. She's going to cosmetology school, so someday she'll own her own business. And she's tall. I know you like the tall ones. And," she added with emphasis, "she goes to church."

Morris bit his tongue. *Great. She's a gangly high school dropout who recently joined a cult. But at least I'll get free haircuts, right?* As dignified as Hattie was, she had a weakness for romance. Morris had often observed paperback novels on her desk, forlorn lovers clasped in fevered embrace on the covers. He knew she wouldn't rest until he found a nice girl to settle down with. He glanced involuntarily at Sheri, then hoped with all his might that Hattie hadn't noticed.

"I hate to disappoint you," he lied through his smiling teeth, "but I happen to like life as a bachelor."

Her mouth twitched with the strain of suppressed laughter. "You and I both know that's not true," she said. "What sane man likes coming home to a cold, empty apartment every evening? Even the good Lord said it's not right for man to be alone."

The bell sounded its dull, electronic chime to signal the start of the school day, and Morris sighed with relief.

"You've got me there," he admitted. "I can't argue with that kind of authority." He helped her off the sofa, and they moved with the others into the hall.

"So you're free Saturday?"

He stalled. "Actually . . . I already have a date for Saturday." Her eyes lit up like those of a bloodhound on a rabbit trail, and he could have slapped himself. *That's what you get for lying to this dear woman.*

"Anyone I know?"

"Um." He blanched. The hall was swarming with kids. "It's Sheri, actually," he said, praying that she wasn't within earshot.

"Aha! Good choice, young man. I definitely approve."

Hattie wagged her finger at him and laughed as she walked off to class, her sensible pumps clicking smartly down the hall.

He relaxed, feeling like a sentenced inmate receiving the governor's call. His last encounter with Hattie's romantic sensibilities was unfortunately still a vivid memory. A stellar sense of humor or heart of gold would have easily compensated for what the young lady lacked in looks, but she turned out to be desperately wanting for a personality as well. Hattie had promised him that she was charming, but as he squirmed in a booth at his favorite little bistro, all he could wonder was whether or not the men's room had a window. He could leave some money, slip into the night, and no one would be the wiser. He felt fairly certain his date wouldn't notice. She'd still be droning on about her ex-boyfriend's insensitivity and her plans to be Miss America.

The worst part had been breaking the news to Hattie. "She'll make a fine wife for someone," he reported, feeling like a whipped dog. "Just not for me. "

A figure darted toward him through the throng of children, pausing to giggle at his kneecap and give his pant leg a vicious tug before disappearing down the art hall in a rush of air. Morris grinned and followed the vanishing imp. A smothered giggle sounded from a doorway on the right. He proceeded on silent feet, relishing every moment of the game. She might be smaller, she might even be faster, but he had the advantage of patience. Unable to bear the suspense, she poked her head around the corner. Two shining black pigtails, two shining dark eyes.

"Aaarrrgg!" Morris growled. The phantom shrieked with delight as Morris planted his hands on her shoulders and motored her down the hall. "Sophie Ling," he clucked. "You're going to be late for class if you don't hurry."

Sophie laughed and shook her head, clearly not concerned, and Morris couldn't help but envy her. To be seven and carefree again . . .

"I'm bringing my dad to parent-teacher night tomorrow," she announced.

"I'll be there to help set up," Morris replied. "I'd like to meet him."

They reached Sheri's room as the first grade was lining up to march in.

"Morris!" a little boy cried, flapping his parka-clad arms. "Look at my new coat!"

"Morris! Morris! I got an A on my math test!" A small fist thrust a crumpled paper proudly into the air.

"I got a gecko for my birthday!"

Each child had something to share, and Morris listened attentively, giving congratulatory high fives and consoling pats on the shoulder where they were needed.

The line stopped abruptly as the first children made their way into Sheri's newly decorated room. They floated to their desks in a dreamlike state, mouths open and eyes glistening in the light of a thousand stars. Sheri smiled at him over the children, and Morris felt his lungs constrict.

"That's the effect I was going for," she said.

What he wouldn't have given for a glib reply. The world and all its glory seemed a small price for the right words to say. Instead he tugged on Sophie's pigtails and scooted her into place.

"Sorry, kiddo," he said, "looks like you're last in line."

She craned her neck to look up at him, her soft, black brows drawn together, puzzling over what she thought was obvious. "I'm glad," she said. "It's good to let other people go first."

Morris could count on one hand the number of times in his life he had shed actual tears, the last time being fifteen years ago at his father's funeral. But honestly, sometimes the things sweet Sophie said, so earnest and sincere, made him want to cry.

❖ ❖ ❖

Morris pulled insistently on the splintered shaft of wood. *Why* yank! *won't* yank! *this* yank! *budge?* On the fifth yank it wriggled loose from its confines and popped easily out of the broken VCR. He studied it carefully. It was flaking a distressed yellow paint, just as he thought. He set the evidence aside and turned his attention to the dissected machine and the myriad mystery pieces scattered over the table. That many parts meant that the VCR was either very cheap or very expensive; he couldn't tell which. Whatever the case, it would need to be handled with care. It was almost time for recess when the last unwieldy spring was bent back into place and the VCR whirred to life.

Morris handed it gingerly to Janet, the stern school librarian, with a warning. "Try to keep the kids from jamming pencils in there."

She pursed her thin lips, raised her crayoned eyebrows, and nodded politely. "Thank you, Mr. Jackson."

With nothing else pressing, he headed to the playground to set out bases for the daily kickball game. There was quite a rivalry brewing among the boys, and every recess was a new adventure in teaching them how to keep it a friendly one. Morris officiated the games on occasion, watching carefully to make sure everyone followed the golden rules of sportsmanship. He smiled guiltily at the thought of his Saturday basketball games at the city courts. Thank goodness the kids couldn't see him there.

A stiff wind channeled through the maze of the city's skyscrapers until it was reduced to a cold but gentle breeze across the playground. The early April sun shone steadily between the clouds to warm his back as he walked, and the ground was slowly thawing, soft in spots beneath his feet. A pearl-white crocus nosed its way through the earth to stretch in the dazzling sunlight, grains of soil still clinging to the petals. He drew a breath of satisfaction. The world was a beautiful place after all.

He was pushing home plate into the grass when a glint of silver caught his eye, a dull sliver of light so thin and momentary he wondered if he had imagined it. One of the kids must have lost a necklace in the field. He felt for the hidden treasure with his hand but jumped back as a fiery pain licked up his forearm. A bright thread of blood spread across the knuckle of his middle finger and trickled toward his nail. What was that? A nail? A knife? Surely none of the kids would bring a knife to school. He shivered, faintly nauseated by the unexpected wound, and bent again to the grass.

The needle looked strangely undisturbed, perched on a leaf with its glittering tip pointed up like a rocket into the still morning sky. Morris fell back in horror, a cold shudder running up his spine to the base of his skull. He lifted his dripping hand to his face, blood trickling toward his wrist. *God, no!* Awful possibilities flashed through his mind. He couldn't have . . . it couldn't be. Surely, if he had touched the needle, he would have knocked it from that frail leaf with his groping hand. But if he hadn't touched it, what had cut him? He scanned the ground, forcing his mind from panicked thoughts of death and disease. Six inches to the left of the needle was a clump of grass, frozen by the morning frost into sharp spines. Rapidly drying on one of its razor points was a rusty drop of blood.

He had come within inches of plunging his hand into a used drug needle. He staggered to his feet and sank onto a nearby bench, sick at the thought of what he could have contracted. His mind raced as he dabbed his wounded finger on a scrap of paper fished out of his pocket. What if he hadn't been there to find it? What if he had still been inside, trying to pry a pencil from a VCR, when the kids had come out to play? They would have stormed the field, rounding the bases, sprinting breathlessly toward home, missing the needle by a fraction of an inch. Connor Parker would have sent the red ball sailing with one mighty kick, and sliding into home plate, the needle could have, would have wriggled into his small leg as he cried out in pain.

Jabbering voices broke into his thoughts. Kids were flooding the playground. As he carefully scooped the needle onto a plastic base, he could have sworn he saw the glittering residue of some junkie's heroin fix lingering inside.

"Sorry, guys," he said as he took the big rubber ball from the group of boys flocking toward him. "No kickball today. Stay off the field."

A chorus of groans rose from the group.

"C'mon, Morris, why?" redheaded James Baker asked, looking crestfallen.

"Sorry, Big J," Morris said. "Absolutely no one goes on the field today, all right?"

They reluctantly agreed and turned away, muttering complaints under their collective breath.

He needed help. He couldn't stand there with dirty drug paraphernalia in his hands guarding the field while who-knew-what other treasures lurked in the grass.

Pete Goreman, a fourth grade teacher, was overseeing a fierce tetherball match across the yard.

"Pete!" Morris yelled, waving urgently with his free hand. "Pe-e-e-ete!"

Pete heard his name and came running, his face beaming from behind his glasses. "Hey, Morris! What's going on?" He stuck out his hand.

"Sorry, Pete. I'd shake your hand if it weren't for my precious cargo." He held out home plate for his friend's inspection.

Pete opened his mouth, but no words came out. He shut it, then opened it again.

"Goreman, you look like a goldfish!" Morris teased halfheartedly. "I found this beauty in the kickball field. I've got to go alert the powers that be. Could you make sure none of the kids come anywhere near the grass?"

Pete nodded, looking as if he might throw up. "What kind of world do we live in when kids can't even play outside without stepping on drug needles and catching HIV or hepatitis?"

Morris wondered the same thing. His stomach rolled into a hard little knot as he carried home plate toward the principal's office.

Chapter 5

The late-night talk show host cackled at his own joke, running his hands through his hair and fiddling with his tie. The cameras panned across the roaring audience and halted at a group of beefy, buzz-cut marines, who jumped from their seats and pumped their fists in the air. Back onstage, poodles trimmed into huge snowballs of fur nudged soccer balls into makeshift goals. More laughter. The audience was hysterical, and all the while the band pumped out a jazzy tune. The grainy images flashed across the small TV in rapid succession, casting a flickering light into the otherwise dark room.

Morris lay stretched out on his old plaid couch, his feet dangling a foot past the end as he tried to sleep. Insomnia had never been a problem for him. In fact, he couldn't remember the last time he had been awake for more than a few moments once his weary head hit the pillow. But this night sleep was a lost cause. He sat up and swung his feet to the floor. A commercial for a popular nighttime sleep aid pranced across the television. A woman in a lace nightgown yawned and snuggled seductively against her pillow. "Recommended by four out of five doctors!" she chirped drowsily.

Were you wearing that nightgown when they recommended it? He couldn't help but wonder.

His left leg twitched in violent spasms against the wooly cushions. Morris was ready for sleep. His body yearned for it. The room was cool and dark, his bladder was empty, and he hadn't had any caffeine that day except for the grainy coffee in the teachers' lounge that morning. *Fine.* He lay down again, pummeled the unwilling cushions into shape, and squashed one under his head. *Fine, I'll just go to sleep then.* He willed the stubborn muscles in his face to relax, but he couldn't close his eyes. He knew what he would see. He couldn't for the life of him forget the ugliness of the needle in the grass, the analysis from the police lab that confirmed everyone's worst fears, or what might have happened if he hadn't been there to find it.

Who would have stumbled across that tiny rocket of death? Who would have fallen on it with a yelp of surprise? Which child would have been dragged before his doctor a year later to find the reason for his pale and wasting frame? Which parents would have been told with unbearable gravity that their child was dying?

Six inches. Six inches to the left and I'd already be dying the short, unhappy life of a eunuch.

Like the mangled VCR he had fixed earlier in the day, his tired brain came obstinately back to one frame, one flickering image, again and again. It was Vern's face. The vacancy of his eyes and the drooping corners of his mustache and his mouth as the needle was laid before him. *Maybe there's a pencil jammed in my ear.* He was finding it hard not to feel a little cynical.

❖ ❖ ❖

Vern Hall had been the principal of Quiley Heights Elementary School for just over a year, but he was as perfect a fit to the place as his worn leather cowboy boots were to his feet. He was a little older, presumably somewhere in the neighborhood of Hattie's age, although it was all a guess since no one knew how old Hattie was. His tall, wiry frame could be seen bounding through the halls, crowned with its mop of blond hair sprinkled liberally with gray. The teachers affectionately referred to him as "the Marlboro man" because of his lean, sun-weathered face. He was also much stronger than his thin frame belied. Morris, on one of his occasional trips to the weight room of the neighboring high school, found a group of wide-eyed, whispering teenagers huddled around a sweaty, red-faced Vern benching three hundred pounds.

There was a freshness about Vern that Morris loved, which made him feel as though every conversation was a brief escape to somewhere wild. He spent as much time as he could in the classrooms with the kids and gladly wrestled with the school board for every desperately needed dollar of funding, a task he wryly referred to as "roping the three-headed calf." Everyone liked Vern, even if he did have a painfully corny sense of humor.

"Mr. Jackson!" he had grunted with his usual glee as Morris entered his office that afternoon. "How's the best custodian in the city? Aren't you supposed to be out on the playground?" He paused before delivering the punch line. "Those kids aren't *scrubbing* you the wrong way, are they?" He chuckled to himself. "Get it? Scrubbing?" He noted the lack of response and cleared his throat. "It's just a little cleaning humor."

Morris sighed. "Uh, Vern, we've got a real problem." He

slid home plate across the wide oak desk and cursed himself for being cowardly. Why did he feel like a kid caught passing a note in class?

Vern stared blankly at the needle while a long moment passed in silence. Morris wondered if he should explain. He opened his mouth but shut it again as Vern drooped over the desk. The corners of his mouth hung limply, and Morris thought for a moment that he might cry. The principal suddenly looked his age.

"I found it in the grass on the kickball field just before recess," Morris explained, flexing his stinging knuckle.

Vern reached for the phone. "A friend at the police precinct owes me a favor," he growled. "Maybe he knows who hangs out in this neighborhood, which druggie left this on our lawn."

That's unlikely. Morris flopped down in one of the padded chairs reserved for the visiting parents of misbehaving students and waited until Vern finished barking into the receiver. He had to get something off his chest.

"I feel like this is my fault in some way," he confessed, staring at the cut on his hand.

Vern hopped from his seat.

"Don't think that, Morris!" he fumed. "You couldn't have kept this from happening even if you had a whole team of janitors combing the grass every morning. It's just the way of the world."

✣ ✣ ✣

Morris stared wide-eyed into the couch. The fibers tickled his face in the deep darkness as Vern's words sounded in his mind. The way of the world?

Nice going, God. Great place You've got here. Next time You're passing out pain and suffering, could You lay off the little kids and make sure the people who deserve it get some?

He rolled over to face the TV. *The Late Late Show.* Had an hour passed already? More jokes about the president, more dog tricks, and an interview with Hollywood's latest starlet, a bleached blonde giggler there to show off her latest plastic surgery. He struggled to pay attention as a restless sleep finally overcame him.

❖ ❖ ❖

He gazed up at the shimmering treetops and gulped the pure, sweet air, the memory of rousing from paradise to the misery of the waking world grating briefly at his nerves. Waking up from those dreams was like crashing from a gloriously blinding high. He wasn't sure he could stand another glimpse of perfection, another dulling hangover in the gray morning light as he ached for the imaginary. A breeze kicked up, lifting his frustration with a pleasant shiver. There were no drug dealers or diseases or dying children here. Nothing and no one to worry about.

Morris found himself in a grove of sheltering trees, drawn into the murmuring shadows by leaves that fluttered like a flock of silver birds. He crushed his thumb into a mossy trunk, relishing the faint spice that took him back to his mother's herb garden in their tiny, sunny yard. *Sage . . . juniper . . . mint.* The smells of home filled him with a sudden desperation. He wanted to climb that tree, to rub the bark against his face and see the silver cloud, to know with all the fervor of a treeless childhood the wonder of the growing thing. He hooked an elbow around the lowest branch and swung his leg toward the trunk but dropped to the ground in sudden fear, an unspoken warning still stinging his palms. Those trees were not for climbing.

"They're keeping watch," he murmured, backing out of the shadows. "Guarding against . . . what are they guarding against?"

Surely, there's nothing in this perfect world to be afraid of.

An unexpected blast knocked him to the grass as he stepped from beneath the shade, picking him over with a ruthless hand. He scrambled up and sought refuge in the lush foliage of a field, smoothing the memory of the chilling gale from his skin. Once again he was warm and content, never dreaming that a lesser life existed. Morris set his sights on a row of rounded foothills in the distance and broke into a run.

Fragrant meadows slipped by beneath his feet in a sea of flowing flowers and grass. The sun burst from the horizon, scattering a comforting glow through the clouds as he watched it from beneath a sheltering hand. *The sun rises and sets here too. At least my dreams are realistic.* He lowered his hand and followed the sun from behind a cloud. *Why doesn't this hurt? A sun that doesn't burn? What next?* He pulled a thorny thistle from the ground and raked the stem across his wrist, laughing at the tickle of soft purple plume. *Of course, this is a perfect world.* That meant no weariness and no pain. *No sickness, no hunger, no death.* He leaned against the trunk of a fragrant tree, twirling the flower in his hands. *No car wrecks, no widows, no helpless little boys.*

A ripe, red fruit slipped from the tree into his open palm. He laughed and bit into the tangy treat. Perfection wore on him very well.

"I'm thirsty." He sighed, barely voicing the thought before the roar of rushing water filled his ears. He scrambled around an outcropping of rock and skittered to a halt, kicking up clouds of soft brown sand. A froth-white waterfall thundered from high above, pouring into the boiling mists of an inlet.

The earth shook and the water deafened as, for the first time in his life, Morris felt wonderfully small.

He cupped the water in his palms. Drops clung to his fingers, flashing like diamonds as they fell to the sand. His limbs felt light, buoyed by the sparkling cold as the water filled his mouth. He plunged his head into the bay. The quiet and the cold were an exquisite pain beneath the surface, the falls rumbling dimly above. Schools of small yellow fish turned in unison nearby, darting back and forth toward the shore, while a pod of dolphins played in the distance, chortling in an endless game. He shook the water from his ears and fell back onto the sand, a soothing warmth invading every fiber of his being.

This is joy. He groaned with the delight of perfect freedom. *Pure joy.* The earth pressed warm against his back, the sky beckoned from a depth of blue. He wanted to fly, to soar like the birds that leaped from the rocks of the waterfall into the lifting winds. *Maybe I can. Maybe here I can fly.*

A strange sound derailed his thoughts, slicing through the din of the falls like a flash of sunlight. He cupped his ear as it came again. An animal. *A monkey.* He leaped up, shaking the soft sand from his clothes, and jogged toward a hill on his right. The sound came again, a bright vine of laughter weaving through the trees. It was decidedly human and female no less, and in a clearing in the distance movement flickered through the trees. He fell to the grass and slunk toward the clearing on his shins and elbows, surprised by his desire to see before being seen. Who could it be? The falls crashed behind him. The laughter stopped, and his ears rang in the relative quiet of the birds and the wind in the trees. He wedged his long frame between a boulder and a mound of grass and peered into the clearing, where a man and a woman stood locked in a passionate embrace.

Morris wondered for a moment if they were human after all. *Wild creatures.* They clung to each other in a tangle of graceful limbs and gleaming hair. *Wild and fresh.* She lifted her eyes to his, and a ray of light shot through them as through deep water. The man's voice rolled softly into her ear, and her answer was melodic and bright. His eyes flashed with gladness as he reached for her, and Morris looked away.

She pulled back at last with a playful swat and turned to a nearby tree where fat ruby fruits dangled in the branches. Together they gathered a sweet and sticky bounty, eating hungrily as they filled their arms. *Enough of this.* Morris kneaded his cramped legs. *I should at least introduce myself.* He stepped from behind the rock and cleared his throat. They didn't miss a beat, fruit snapping from its stems as it fell into their outstretched arms. Dismayed, he coughed again, forcing a rough syllable at the end. Still they worked. Morris shrugged. He didn't want to scare them—for all he knew they thought they were the only ones in the orchard—but it seemed best to be direct. He stepped into the clearing.

"Hello?" No reaction. "Hello?"

Were they deaf? He stepped in front of the man and offered what he hoped was a nonthreatening smile and a wave. The man didn't see him at all but rather looked through him, and Morris was forced to duck to avoid having his eye gouged out as the man reached for another piece of fruit.

This is bizarre. He rocked back on his heels uneasily. *Are they ghosts? Am I a ghost?*

The woman jumped back with a shriek, spilling her heavy crop. She pointed into the branches, chattering rapidly to the man. He parted the branches with a frown, laying a protective hand on her arm. A tense moment passed, dropped fruit wobbling awkwardly toward Morris's feet, until a tiny lizard leaped out from the center of the tree and landed lightly on the branch before their eyes. The man laughed at the sprightly, jeweled creature as it hopped from twig to twig. The woman scooped it into her hand and cooed as it flickered its minute tongue and rolled its little eyes. She offered it a bit of fruit, and it began to dance and wag its twig of a happy tail.

They laughed, and Morris laughed with them at the most amazing animal he had ever seen. It smacked its lips daintily and winked a round, black eye as it shuffled through a rainbow of colors. They watched in awe as the snippet of a reptile flushed with vibrant green, indigo, scarlet, and flashing gold. Each color followed in bright fingers from the tip of the creature's tiny tail to its sweetly curved beak, prompting a prolonged shiver between each shade. The woman stroked it lovingly with one last pat before she bent to gather her spilled harvest. She smiled meaningfully at her mate, and together they turned toward the heart of the garden. Morris watched wistfully as they disappeared into the deepening shade of the trees. It was like watching the last guests leave from a wonderful party, and suddenly he felt alone. They had filled him with a kind of happiness, a sense of belonging, he had never known.

A subtle rustling in the leaves turned his head. It was the lizard, its four claws wrapped tightly around a branch, staring intently at him. Something wasn't right. It wasn't dancing anymore or smiling but clinging to the branch and panting as if it were in pain. Morris backed away from the tree and tried to shake the feeling that the creature was calculating a leap for his jugular. Its tiny nostrils flared as something crawled from the back of its throat with a wisp of smoke: a guttural hiss that scattered the birds and stilled the air. It was then Morris felt it, a suffocating dread, irrational and cold, which lifted the hair from his arms. Something terrible was coming.

Shadows bled from the trees and seeped up from the grass, dragging night into the garden. The heaving lizard doubled in size, the branches groaning beneath its weight. It doubled in size again and again as the soft hide darkened to the color of dried blood, and scales crackled as spines broke through the leathery hide. Morris backed into the boulder, groping at its granite face.

"No!" he gasped. Where was his peace? His joy? Fear burned through his limbs as the creature thundered through the branches to the ground with a sickening thud. It garbled toward him with a seizing hiss, gnashing its teeth, feeding on his fear.

Oh, God. What is it? He gagged as the air filled with the stench of rotting flesh, his lips stinging with vomit and blood. *Oh, God. I'm dying. I'm dying.* The beast slouched toward him one leg at a time and cracked its lower jaw.

"Aarrhhhhh," it hissed. "Morris!" It snarled, a demon in the darkness.

Morris wedged his head beneath the rock. *Kill me. It's going to . . .* He couldn't breathe. His lungs were filling. The smell of death burned around him. *I don't want to die.*

The creature roared. The earth shook as it charged. He yelped at the searing heat as darkness fell, and he knew nothing more.

Chapter 6

Morris slumped over the kitchen table and waited for the water to boil. It was five o'clock in the morning, but he couldn't sleep. Not after that. He wondered if he would ever sleep again. He nursed a few drops of Visine into his grainy eyes, flinching slightly as the liquid burst over his stinging pupils, and wondered what the rest of the dark city was doing. The teakettle puffed, quickly building to an off-key scream. He snatched it from the burner and glanced nervously at the door.

Feeling particularly miserly one Saturday afternoon, he had bought the kettle at a garage sale. It wasn't until he got it home that he discovered the warped lip of the spout . . . and the bloodcurdling whistle. Two policemen had nearly broken down his door when a nervous neighbor called the cops with a domestic disturbance charge. It took a demonstration of the kettle to convince the cops that it was his teapot, not a woman, screaming.

He dug a box of tea out of the cupboard, desperate for a caffeine fix. Three tortured hours of sleep weren't much to go on. He wondered with a sigh, as he watched the amber tea bleed from the bag into its boiling bath, what it would take to stop the dreams.

What was that? He stiffened. It came again, a distinct creaking of the floorboards in his bedroom. He pulled a meat cleaver from the wooden knife block on the counter, then slammed it back down.

"Get a grip." He rubbed his eyes. "Your floorboards always creak."

In a moment of sleep-deprived weakness, he considered seeking professional help at one of the free counseling clinics scattered throughout the city. He envisioned himself stretched out on a leather sofa, spilling his guts to a nodding, scribbling shrink. The bespectacled little man would hem and haw and clear his throat.

"Well, Morris," he would say, "I think your troubles stem from the fact that you were potty-trained incorrectly."

No thank you. Even worse, he might end up in one of those group therapy sessions where everyone sat in a lopsided circle and listened to crack addicts recount with relish their dreams of flying. He gulped the tea down, chasing it with a bitter glass of grapefruit juice.

No, he wasn't desperate enough to visit a psychiatrist. Not on account of some piddling dreams. He was an intelligent, rational young man, and he would deal with his problems in his own way. He began to feel better as he pulled on his jeans and tucked in his button-down shirt. Of course he could deal with those dreams. After all, he was Morris Jackson, and he wasn't afraid of anything. People came to *him* for help. He pulled the front door shut behind him and fumbled with the keys.

The ride to work was blessedly uneventful, and although he was a little slower than usual and breathed a little harder climbing the hill, Morris still arrived an hour early. The school was dark and quiet with a mausoleum-like quality to the musty air. He could hear the furnace kicking on and the air vents chuffing to life all over the building. What to do first?

Well, I guess I could clean out the supply closet.

The closet was narrow but deep and tall with shelves lining the walls and every inch of floor space cluttered with buckets and brooms. A thin chain brushed against his ear in the dark. He gave it a tug, and one solitary bulb sputtered to life. Morris scanned the shelves for the most potent cleaning solvent he could find and finally chose a plastic jug with a skull and crossbones on the front and a label of health warnings in four languages on the back. He pulled on his industrial-grade rubber gloves with a snap and grabbed a sponge as the light above his head went out with a brief sizzle. He leaned his tired forehead against the shelf in the darkness.

Something skittered by his foot. He thought of the mousetraps he'd set out a few weeks ago, how he painstakingly wedged a cheese curl under each of the trap wires. *Must be a big one.* An unpleasant tingle zipped across his chest. He started to make his way back out of the closet when he heard it: a long, deliberate hiss behind him.

This was no dream. He was pinned in a dark closet with some *thing* clawing at him from behind. In a burst of strength he fought through the mess, snapping a frailer broom in half and sending buckets sailing, until he floundered into the hall. Propping the door wide open to let in the daylight, he faced the closet again, wielding a dustpan like a sword. Now he would see exactly what it was. That thing would rue the day it came into his school. He followed the raggedy hiss to the back of the closet and threw down an old towel. Distorted shadows swung over him as he lifted the flat end of the dustpan above his head. His muscles twitched with anticipation. *This is it.* He yanked the towel away with his free hand and brought the pan crashing down with the other. *Clang!* The jolt of metal on metal vibrated through his arm as he searched for an oozing, scaly hide.

It was a faucet. A hose hookup near the floor that he rarely used was sputtering and bubbling droplets of water into a slow puddle on the concrete. The dustpan fell to the floor with a clatter. Morris cranked the faucet shut and sat down on an overturned bucket, his head heavy in his hands. It was official. He was losing his mind.

He cleaned up what he could of the mess he had created and left the rest for another day. Thank goodness he was the only one with a key to that closet. He didn't know how he could have explained the disorder to anyone else. Fighting off an evil reptilian beast wasn't exactly a plausible excuse. Maybe he did need counseling.

High-pitched voices bounced through the empty hallways as the first children arrived. Time to start another day.

He found the kids wiggling in their regimented lines in the gym, shuffling their feet and scrubbing the lipstick stains left by their mothers from their cheeks and foreheads as a teacher looked on. Others would join them soon, trickling into their lines until the bell rang and the march to their classrooms began. Several saw him coming and skittered out of line.

"Oowwww," Morris moaned. He staggered toward them, clutching his stomach to ease an invisible pain. A crowd of worried faces closed in on him.

"Morris, what is it?" a little girl queried anxiously.

"Is it your appendix?" asked a boy, too tall for his nine

years. Morris appeared to double over in pain, and the circle closed in on him with cries of "Morris! What's wrong?" There was a moment of tense silence before he rocketed with a roar from the bottom of the pile.

"Gotcha!" he yelled amid the shrieks and laughter. He chased the kids back into line and gave the teacher a mock salute.

"I knew you were faking it," the tall boy said triumphantly.

Morris reached down to ruffle his hair. "Noah, how do you know about appendicitis anyway?" he asked.

Noah grinned. "My mom works in a doctor's office. She talks about that stuff all the time."

A chorus of groans rose from the kids as the bell rang. Morris promised to poke his head out at recess if he had the time, which cheered them up significantly. Thank goodness it didn't take much to keep them content.

❖ ❖ ❖

The morning passed slowly. He trimmed the hedges around the entire building, scrubbed the sinks in the girls' bathrooms, and helped Vern's secretary corner an enormous spider before it was finally time for lunch. Why he was so desperate for the day to end he didn't know. The evening certainly held no fairer prospects.

Out on the playground, spring was making a brave showing. Every day the grass looked a little greener, and the tightly bound buds on the trees swelled a little closer to their bursting point. Kids peeled off their mittens and wrapped their eager palms around monkey bars that no longer bristled with stinging frost, while rubber-soled shoes squawked down the slide and legs pumped at the air through gleaming chains as swingers launched themselves to new heights.

He strolled around the blacktop, watching for anything amiss. In the distance, warning signs on wooden posts dotted the field, which was still off-limits to the kids. It looked unnaturally empty, a lonely testament to the depravity of the world. *Whoa.* He caught himself. *I sound like Vern. That's not how the world works. Not everyone is a depraved murderer or drug dealer or . . . or sinner.*

A huddle of little girls darted back and forth across the concrete yard, giggling in some silly variation of follow-the-leader. First they hopped on one foot with their fingers jammed into their ears, then galloped across the blacktop with their eyes closed. The leader halted abruptly, and they crashed into a pile of hysterical laughter. Morris surveyed the tangled arms and legs, looking for Sophie. If they were having that much fun, she was sure to be involved. She pulled free from the center of the laughing heap and ran to him.

"Morris!" Her curtain of black hair bounced over her shoulders as she came, her round face breathless with excitement. She wore a jacket the color of the cautionary tape looped around the perimeter of the field and a pair of baggy jeans. Morris stepped out to meet her and watched as the inevitable happened just a few feet away. She snagged the toe of her sneaker in her drooping hem and pitched forward. He thrust out one of his long legs to break her fall, and she dived for his knee.

"I almost fell!" she panted, wrapping her arms around his shin.

"You okay?" he asked. She nodded with a giggle. He lifted his free leg and began an awkward march around the yard, while she clung to his leg, shrieking with laughter.

"Okay, kiddo." He plopped her onto a bench. "Morris needs a break."

Sophie ripped open the Velcro pocket on her jacket and fished around inside.

"I made you something," she said as she pulled a folded square of white construction paper from her coat. She smoothed the colorful drawing of flowers and trees across her lap before she handed it to him.

"Thanks, Soph. It's really beautiful. And I know the perfect place to put it."

"You should hang it in a window," she advised. "That way the sun will shine through."

He held it up to the spring sky. "You're right," he said. He followed the lines of translucent wax across the page. "Did you draw this in art class?"

"No, at church. We were supposed to draw pictures of heaven." She swung her legs back and forth beneath the bench. "Everyone else was drawing clouds and angels, but this is what I think heaven will look like."

He tilted his head for a closer look at Sophie's masterpiece. Tall trees, black crayon curls of wind, purple flowers in the grass, a waterfall to the left. He lowered the picture.

"Sophie, who told you what to draw?"

"No one," she said, happily scuffing her tennis shoes green in the grass. "That's just what I want heaven to be like."

Just a coincidence. Some common image lodged in our collective subconscious. That had to be it.

"Who is this?" He pointed to an obviously Asian woman smiling from a hill of spring green grass.

The legs slowed to a gentle rocking. "That's my mom," Sophie said quietly. "She died when I was three, but I know she's in heaven and she's happy."

He nodded and swallowed against the lump that threatened his throat. Why did little girls like Sophie have to lose their moms? He pointed to the bearded figure next to Mrs. Ling. "Who's this?"

She giggled. "That's Jesus." She said it so convincingly he almost laughed.

"Of course." He smiled. "It's Jesus." *What a trusting kid. She really believes that.*

"Jesus died so my mom could go to heaven and be with Him," she continued.

Wow, time to change the topic already. "Sophie, how did your mom die?" he asked.

She stopped swinging her legs abruptly and turned on the bench to face him, pulling her knees up under her chin.

"She had leukemia. I don't remember her very well."

The gruesome word sounded strange coming from one so small.

"My dad says she was beautiful."

Morris cleared his throat. "I bet she was. You know," he continued, hardly believing his own voice, "my father died when I was ten. He was driving home from work in a snowstorm." He could see it all again: the car careening toward their house, the splintered telephone pole, the shattered glass. *Spare the kid the details.* "He was killed in an accident."

Sophie gave him the understanding nod of one who had felt the blow and knew the sting.

"My mom missed him very much." He didn't know what else to say.

Sophie watched the other kids on the playground blankly for a moment.

"Sometimes my dad still cries when he talks about my mom," she whispered, "but he says it's not God's fault. God doesn't make bad things happen."

Morris couldn't have explained it, but that made him

fighting mad. Who was this guy to indoctrinate his little daughter with such trash? He clenched his jaw. If God wasn't responsible, who else? *She's just a kid. She doesn't know any better.* He reached around to pat the back of her head.

"I think your dad must love you very much," he said.

She brightened again. "He's coming to the meeting tonight. You can meet him."

"I can't wait, Soph." The tinny trill of the recess whistle sounded across the school yard. "Time for class, Miss Ling."

Sophie hopped to her feet and scampered off to line up with her classmates.

❖ ❖ ❖

Before he knew it, Morris was helping Hattie scoot kids out the door and gathering lunch boxes, folders, and mittens into the lost-and-found box. When the last scarf was rescued from the cafeteria floor and the dust bunnies brushed from its orange yarn fringe, he locked the school and dashed home for a bite of dinner. *I don't have much time.* He looked at his watch. *A sandwich will have to do. Maybe roast beef with Swiss.*

An hour and a half later he was giving the gym a final sweeping and wondering what Sheri was up to. She was probably combing her beautiful hair or sinking her beautiful teeth into dinner or slipping her beautiful arms into a jacket and heading out the door. He hadn't seen her all day, and there was something he needed to ask her. With a little luck he would catch her later that night.

A string of headlights crept up the street toward the parking lot, rivaling the streetlights and washing all but a few stars from the city sky. Families pulled into parking spots, climbed out of their cars, and made their way toward the building.

Most of the teachers were still crowded into the lounge, fluffing their hair and straightening their shirts and knocking back one last cup of coffee before meeting the parents of their best and worst students.

Morris milled around in the entryway, opening the doors for people and greeting the rambunctious kids. Some of the parents knew him, and they greeted him with smiles and warm handshakes. Connor Parker's father slapped him heartily on the back.

"Morris, I couldn't drag Connor to school if it weren't for you," he said with a laugh. "I hear you're a master kickball referee."

Morris just smiled. "It keeps me young." He turned to ask Noah's mom about her new job when he heard the pounding of small feet from behind. He turned just in time to see Sophie launching herself in his direction, pigtails streaming out behind. Noah's mother gasped, but Morris just bent and plucked Sophie out of the air.

"Sophie, how did you know I would turn around in time to catch you?" he asked.

"I just knew you would," she laughed. "My dad's here," she said. "He wants to meet you."

Coming toward them with a grin like a toothpaste commercial was Morris's Bible reader from the subway. *Of course.* Sophie and her father shared the same smile, the same melting eyes. *Now the Bible makes sense. He's some kind of religious nut.* He smiled hesitantly. *Does he recognize me?*

Sophie grabbed her father's hand and towed him over.

"Morris," she said in her most grown-up voice, "this is my dad, Dr. Ling. Dad, this is Morris. He's the janitor."

"Actually," Morris said, putting out his hand, "I prefer custodial engineer."

Dr. Ling laughed and shook his hand. "Please, call me Ken." He smiled sheepishly. "Sophie's the only person in the world who calls me 'Dr. Ling.'" He rolled his daughter's abundant hair into a ball and plopped it on top of her head. "Isn't that right, Sophie?"

She shook her hair free and squeezed his hand. "Wait here," she instructed. "I'm going to find Miss Wallace." She darted off down the hall.

Morris relaxed. If Ken recognized him, he was pretending not to.

"So," he nudged the conversation along, "Sophie never mentioned that you were a doctor."

"Actually, I'm not a medical doctor."

Please don't tell me you're a shrink.

"I've got a doctorate in divinity."

Divinity? Isn't that a type of candy? Despite his efforts, Morris felt the question flash across his own face.

"I'm the pastor of Community Church downtown," Ken explained.

Morris feigned interest. *What's the deal? I can't escape these guys.* He gave Ken another look. He seemed far too laid-back to be a pastor. Was he waiting until later to whip out the ol' Bible and start thumping? Plus, he had a decent sense of humor, and he was a snappy dresser.

"You're really a pastor?" He hoped he didn't sound too surprised.

Ken suppressed a smile. "Afraid I am. It's the church on the corner of Lincoln and Helm."

Morris knew the one. It was an old stone building in the center of the city with stained-glass windows and iron steeples. They ran a homeless shelter up the street and hosted AA meetings on the weekends.

Ken was trying his hardest not to look amused, but his eyes betrayed him. "Let me guess," he said. "I'm either too young or too normal, right?"

Morris exhaled a laugh. "Well, both actually," he said. "It's just that I've met some pastors in the past who weren't so . . . normal."

Ken was suddenly serious. "Not all preachers are nut jobs, Morris." The corners of his mouth twitched. "Just most of us."

By the time Sophie came skipping back, Morris was very much at ease. He liked Ken. It was hard not to.

Hattie appeared before the growing crowd of parents with a gracious smile.

"Ladies and gentlemen," she said with a practiced flourish, "welcome to Quiley Heights Elementary School's thirty-second annual parent-teacher night."

The crowd murmured its approval.

"If you'll follow the hallway to your right," she continued, "you will find your child's classroom and teacher. After the conferences there will be a time to meet our principal, Mr. Vern Hall, in the gym." The chatting crowd funneled into the hallway, leaving Morris alone with a familiar twinge of longing.

He grabbed the vacuum from the closet, raking over the clumps of dried mud the parents had tracked in with a vigor he hoped would redirect his thoughts. Wandering down to the cafeteria later on, he realized with a sigh that although he didn't want to leave, there was no legitimate reason for him to stay. His stomach seized at a vision of his shadowy apartment and dark bedroom. Who knew what might be lurking in his subconscious, waiting for his head to hit the pillow before it pounced? He cracked his knuckles and turned to other thoughts. He hadn't seen Sheri all day. Was she avoiding him?

Am I that pathetic? She's not even my girlfriend, yet I can't go a day without seeing her?

"Hey."

He whipped around. Sheri's voice, quiet as it was, had spooked him. He cleared his throat and lowered his eyes from her high-beam smile. She was glowing like a lantern.

"Don't tell me you're done with your conferences already."

"Mine didn't take long." She sighed happily. "I've got fabulous kids."

He sank a string of quarters into the pop machine against the wall, handed her one of the Cokes that came thundering out, and sat down.

"Join me?" he asked, mustering all the class he could with his knees jammed against the underside of the kid-sized table. She slid in across from him, absentmindedly tapping the top of her can.

"I hope I'm doing this right," she said thoughtfully.

"Here, let me help," he said. "You just pull up on that aluminum ring at the top and—"

"Morris! I know how to open a pop can!" She leaned over and cuffed his ear, less exasperated than amused. "I'm talking about teaching."

"Sheri," he said, "that's almost laughable. How can you think you're anything but an amazing teacher? Those kids love you."

"That's just it," she moaned. "Maybe they like me too much. Maybe I'm not enough of a disciplinarian." She tapped dully at the aluminum. "Maybe I don't challenge them enough."

He gently took the can from her hands and opened it.

"I think you worry too much," he said, silencing her protest with a hand, "and I know you don't give yourself enough credit. You're an excellent teacher, and somewhere buried in that pretty head of yours you know it."

She shrugged, the prelude to a smile playing at the corners of her lips.

"I guess I can't argue with that." She tipped her head to the side. "But speaking of worry, I'm beginning to worry about you. You look awfully tired."

"I haven't been sleeping that well," he said, waving off her concern. "I've been having these bizarre dreams." *Why am I telling her this?*

"Re-ally?" She nestled her chin into her hands. "What happens in these dreams?"

"Well . . ." He stalled, knowing that there was no way out. Now that she knew, she would hound him until he caved. *What a way to die.* He jumped in, explaining for the first time the orchard and the happy couple, everything but the hideous beast. She didn't need to know that he was a complete lunatic.

She nodded as he spoke. "It's strange," she said when he paused. "It sounds like you're in the Garden of Eden."

He nibbled at his thumbnail. *Of course. The Garden of Eden.* It all made sense: the perfect world . . . the naked couple.

"Actually," he said, scrambling for cover, "I've been watching a lot of those nature shows on the Discovery Channel lately. They've probably been triggering the dreams. I'll just take a sleeping pill tonight. It's no big deal."

She raised a delicate brow, and he knew she wasn't convinced.

"By the way—" *I might as well ask now . . . can't dig myself in any deeper.* "Do you have plans for Saturday night?"

A slow, seductive smile bloomed across her face.

"I don't know," she said. "I'll have to consult my jam-packed social calendar. You know how glamorous my weekends usually are, what with all the yacht racing and club hopping. Why?"

He leaned across the table.

"I make a mean lasagna," he said softly. "Come over for dinner?"

"Morris, you're dangerous." She smiled and tucked her hair behind her ear. "You're too charming for your own good."

"Is that a yes?" He wriggled imperceptibly closer.

"I'll be there."

Chapter 7

The lions were magnificent, long haunches bound in muscle, shoulders squared beneath rippling manes. One nuzzled its whiskered snout between its paws while the other kept watch. Morris ran his hands along their marble backs, sending the picking sparrows into a fright, and paused to read the plaque mounted beneath their silent claws.

"Leoni Stradato, The Resting Lions." He thought of Sheri as the strange words rolled over in his mouth. He saw himself wooing her by candlelight, whispering sweet Italian nothings in her ear as she melted into his arms. Maybe he would join a beginning Italian class at the community center near his apartment.

The sun slid toward the waiting horizon, flaring through the layers of pollution into brilliant oranges and bleeding-heart purples that deepened to shadow in the crevices of the library's granite face. Morris sighed as he climbed the steps. It felt good to be alone. It had been a typical day at work until one of the rowdy third grade boys fell ill and lost his lunch in the hall. Morris had dutifully brought out the odd mixture of pungent orange sawdust that was sprinkled over such incidents and helped the invalid to the nurse.

He drew open the heavy glass doors of the library and instantly felt more educated and interesting than he had in a long time. The smells of dust and ink, of crumbling manuscripts and freshly milled paper hung in the air like a costly incense long in the making. At a nearby table the bleached spine of a new book creaked invitingly in someone's hands. A forest of arms quivered in a busy corner as children crowded around a woman with a picture book in her lap. Morris watched them happily. How many Einsteins were waiting in that crowd of eager children? How many Picassos were studying the colors? Which one of those children would someday discover the cure for cancer? Which future diplomat would bring peace to warring nations? The possibilities were limitless.

"May I help you find something?" asked a bespectacled gentleman from behind the information desk. He couldn't have been more than five feet tall, and Morris wondered if he had always been that . . . petite . . . or if he had shrunk with age.

"Umm . . ." Morris hesitated. He didn't want to be mistaken for one of those overzealous nuts out there. They ruined it for everyone else.

The librarian waited patiently.

"Um, I need to find a Bible, I guess."

"World religions is located on the fourth floor."

Morris thanked him, resisting the unholy urge to pat him on the head, and took off toward the wide winding staircase in the center of the building.

A voice called after him. "I hope you find what you're looking for."

Morris paused with a foot on the first step. *What is that supposed to mean?* He told himself to stop being paranoid and took the steps two at a time.

World religions took only a small portion of space compared to the cavernous world history and natural science departments, but it was still crammed with more books than he could read in a lifetime. Morris peeled off his jacket and set it at one of the tables.

Where was the overwhelming sense of awe, the stirring mystery? Where were the hooded monks chanting up and down the aisles? the clouds of sickly incense? the golden angels and hallelujah choruses? *They could at least get a pipe organ going up here.*

He turned to the stacks of books nearest him. There were manuals for everything from fasting and prayer to ritual cleansing to kosher foods to keeping a properly shorn head. Every fastidious detail of every religion known to man seemed to be covered in some tome. *If this is what it takes to get to heaven, I'm in trouble.*

A shadow wobbled in his peripheral vision, and Morris jumped back as a thick black book toppled from the shelf on his left and crashed to the floor. He picked it up, wondering at its heft and metal-tipped corners. Slashes of fiery red scrawled across the cover. Whatever it was, it wasn't about God, and something told him it wasn't good. He put it down and hurried to the next aisle.

Dozens of Bibles in every size and language crowded the shelves. *And I thought finding a Bible would be hard.* Were they all the same thing? He selected a battered paperback that looked vaguely modern with a rainbow splashed across the front and took it back to the table.

If Sheri was right, and he was traipsing through Eden every night while he slept, he needed to know why, and how to stop, and how the story ended. At least he would know what to expect next. From what he remembered, the whole Adam and Eve thing was toward the beginning. He fluttered through the parchment pages until he found Genesis and started to read.

An hour passed. His stomach growled loudly, inviting a look from a young man devouring the Dalai Lama's latest best-seller at a neighboring table, but Morris didn't care. He had intended just to skim through the first few chapters, enough to get the gist of what was going on, but the story proved too absorbing for that.

As he read, his senses were revived by his memories of paradise. He knew what that garden looked like, how the flowers smelled, what the water tasted like. He knew what Adam felt and how Eve laughed, and as he read he saw her again, feeding a sticky bite of fruit to a prancing lizard. A weight settled in the hollow of his stomach as the pieces came together. That hideous reptile from his dreams was supposed to be . . . and it was going to . . . and beautiful Eve would fall for it. In one nanosecond of weakness, she and Adam would bring the garden and the future of the human race crumbling into a pile of bitter ash around them.

It's not fair.

One passage in particular leapt from the page as he read: "By the sweat of your brow you will eat your food until you return to the ground, since from it you were taken; for dust you are and to dust you will return."

Out of nowhere she came, frantically stumbling through

endless drifts of snow. Steam rose from the ruptured radiator of Saul's car as frightened tears froze on Sandra's cheeks.

Morris massaged his jaw and waited for the memory to pass.

He closed the Bible with a groan. "Well," he said to no one in particular—or maybe to God, in case He had taken a coffee break from running the universe to eavesdrop—"that's the stupidest thing I've ever heard." He waited for the ball of fire to fall from heaven and consume him. Nothing.

He carried the Bible back to the shelf where he'd found it, but as he slid it into place he felt unexpectedly awful, almost unbearably sad. That couldn't be all there was to the story. It was one mistake. One infraction against All-Powerful God, and He punishes His creation forever? Was that how it worked? Was that why drug dealers tossed their needles onto children's playgrounds? why the world was rapidly revealing itself to be a lousy place after all? why his father died on a bed of broken glass?

Morris leaned into the shelf and closed his eyes. It couldn't be. Maybe he hadn't read it right. Maybe there were codes. He thought he'd heard about something like that once. Morris knew if he wanted his curiosity satisfied he would have to read more. He pulled the Bible from the shelf again and started for the stairs.

❖ ❖ ❖

At home, he stirred the barbecued brisket simmering in his slow cooker and sat down to plan Saturday night's menu. His specialty was chicken cacciatore, or "chicken catch-a-girly" as his mother liked to call it, but he had fixed it for so many girls over the years that it just didn't seem special anymore. Sheri wasn't a vegetarian, so lasagna was a great choice. Lasagna with a tossed salad.

The phone rang, and Morris cradled it against his neck as he spooned the tender beef onto a plate. It was one of the regulars from his Saturday basketball games, a stocky fellow who went by the handle "Congo." Congo was also the name of the gorilla that knew sign language at the zoo, a fact that Morris couldn't help but bring to his attention whenever possible. Congo was never amused.

"You better believe I'll be there," Morris said around a mouthful of brisket. "I wouldn't miss a chance to beat you."

Congo's halfhearted reply was followed by a question.

"Sure," Morris laughed, "you can bring all the friends you want. The more people for me to stomp, the merrier." He held the phone away from his ear as Congo launched into a loud stream of mispronounced threats.

"I'll catch you Saturday," he squeezed in at last and hung up the phone. As he stood over the counter eating, he suddenly realized how tired he was. Even his toes ached. He finished dinner, put the leftovers in Tupperware, left the slow cooker in the sink to soak, and headed to the bathroom for his pre-bed ritual. *It's Thursday. I'd better floss.*

There were lights above his bed and voices yelling from a distance. A woman screamed, her voice muffled and slow. Morris's fingers twitched at his sides, and the muscles around his kneecaps jerked sporadically. He felt himself lifted onto his side and turned over and lifted and turned again with increasing speed as the world flickered around him: sky, grass, sky, grass, and in some disconnected sense he knew he was falling. He landed facedown in a bed of flowers, their pungent spices pulling him from sleep on a golden thread, and opened his eyes to a haze of purple petals that clung to his face and his neck as he pulled himself to his knees and then to his feet. He turned around. He had tumbled down a small mountain in his sleep. *Thank goodness nothing in Eden hurts.*

The sun was flaming high in the blue afternoon sky, and the birds were piping with all their might. Their voices were lilting instead of warbling, falling instead of rising. Did the birds in Eden learn a new song every day? He supposed it made sense. Everything else in the garden was a fresh, living wonder; why not the birds? He folded his arms behind his head and fell back into the pile of petals and fragrant herbs. *I think I'll go back to sleep.* He would have purred if he could.

A strangled sound rose above the swelling refrain of the birds and jerked him from his fragrant cocoon with a shiver. He knew what it was and didn't wait to hear it again but bolted toward the deep shade under a canopy of trees a half mile away. It came again—a choking scream. He ran faster. *This wasn't in the Bible.* The devil serpent was supposed to tempt her, not attack her. *But what else could make her scream like that?*

He was almost there, whipping his long legs through the grass, when an awful thought occurred to him. What did he think he was going to do when he got there? Yell "Geronimo" and jump into the fray? The last time he encountered that thing he had been reduced to a sniveling rag behind a rock. Just the memory of the crushing jaws and razor teeth and claws was enough to stock his nightmares for a month. And the sound it made! He was no coward, but he knew if it hissed at him, if it spoke his name again in that demonic garble from the pit of hell, he'd be running the other way. He slowed to a jog under the weight of a terrible realization. It knew him. That . . . thing had called him by name.

He skirted the wide expanse of foliage on silent feet.

Beneath the trees it was as dark as night, the shadows hiding a beast unlike any he'd ever seen. *Maybe I should leave.*

She screamed again, her voice ragged with panic, and he leaped into the trees. *I have to do something. I can't let it kill her.* The element of surprise was his only hope. He grabbed a branch from the ground. He would catch the beast from behind with one swift blow to the back of the head and beat it senseless. With some serious luck he might even kill it. *I'd be a hero.*

He pushed his way through the tangled vines and branches toward a sobbing sound. That had to be the woman, Eve, but why was she crying? Following the pulse of her voice, he stumbled toward a hedge of flowers, his vision dancing with sunspots as he grappled with the trees.

Then he felt it, slouching toward her in his mind, a dark shadow of horror and hell. He tore at the hedge, ripping open a path through the vines. The shadow moved. He raised the branch to his shoulder, wielding it like a bat as adrenaline coursed through his limbs. *One more step.* The shadow pounced. He charged through the bushes, swinging the branch like an ax. Adam's hair stirred in the breeze of the airborne missile as Morris released the branch with a yelp and crashed to the forest floor. Eve's terrified shriek trailed into laughter as her playmate scooped her up and held her captive above his head.

Morris lay stunned, listening to the branch crash through the trees. There was no beast, no devil, no death. Only a happy couple playing rowdy lovers' games. Eve screamed again as Adam gently tackled her and planted a kiss square on her lips. *Why do I bother?* He dragged himself out of the wrestling couple's path. She had scared him out of his wits, and he had almost brained her precious hubby with a stick! Morris scratched his back against the rough bark of a trunk and waited for the kissing and cooing to mercifully stop. Adam helped Eve to her feet with an exclamation, then jabbered something else and bounded from the trees and out of sight. Eve sighed happily and wandered, singing softly to herself, into the sun. Morris, with nothing better to do, followed.

It was impossible to be angry with those two. They were like children at play, brimming with an energy and intimacy and joy that could only exist in a place like Eden, and something within him cried out for it. *What happened to us?* He plopped down behind her in the grass as she stretched out in the sun and began to braid her long hair. He picked at a tuft of grass while she sang and tried not to think about his own life.

He had plenty of good relationships. There were Sheri and Hattie and Pete and Vern and all of the other teachers at school, and his mother and her husband, William. Even some of his Saturday basketball competitors could be considered companions, if not friends. Then why couldn't he be as happy in the real world as he was in his dreams? If there was nothing missing from his life, why were the mornings so empty and cold? Was God just trying to torment him? *"Look at all you had before you screwed up. A perfect world, perfect relationships with each other, and a perfect relationship with Me." Was that it? Real nice, God. I never pegged You as the type to rub it in.*

Where was God anyway? Wasn't He supposed to be creeping around the garden somewhere? Morris flinched. The thought of God sneaking up behind him scared him to death.

Just then Eve began to babble. Morris looked around, but Adam was nowhere to be seen. Was she talking to God? He strained to hear her. Her voice sounded tight, as though she were answering a question she didn't like being asked. He dragged himself up just behind her. Whoever she was talking to was familiar to her; that much was evident by the tone of her voice. He sat up and peeked over her shoulder, then jumped up with a cry. It was back, and she was playing with it. She was scratching its belly. It smiled at her and stretched happily, blinking its round black eyes in the sun. It rolled over and changed from green to blue with a shiver as she stroked the back of its neck.

Morris stepped away and drew back his foot. One clean shot and he could boot that thing into next week. *Just like kicking a field goal.* Suddenly she leaped to her feet, nodding her head and chattering excitedly. The creature must have spoken to her, although he hadn't heard anything, and apparently it suggested something she found quite agreeable. They took off together, running toward the center of the garden. *What now?* He searched the ground for a sharp stick or large rock as he ran. Who knew when that thing would morph into its wicked alter ego?

They ran for miles, laughing and playing with the animals and plants as they went. The garden closed in thicker and darker around them. Fat vines in shimmering depths of blue wrapped around the trunks of the trees and drooped from their branches while a stream gurgled between their roots, and in the quiet of the forest he heard them slurping gleefully at the water. A cool breeze set the leaves to dancing until they whispered and clattered in one great soughing voice that silenced everything else.

Eve slowed to a walk as the animals grew fewer and the plants and trees even denser around them. Morris picked his way through the knotted roots, crawling ivy, and feathered grass and thrilled at the shade and the pleasant cold. A rabbit skittered across his path. He bent to pick it up and marveled for a moment at its coal-black fur, as soft as silk, and its wide green eyes.

A dim light glimmered on the path ahead. He set the squirming rabbit down and followed the light around a bend until he was forced to shade his eyes. One tree stood alone in a hollow of consuming fire. He fell to his knees. The translucent trunk shifted with a hard, diamond light. The countless leaves beamed with the cold white of a full moon, and a searing fire, brighter than the rest, flickered through the branches. The wind ceased. The woods fell silent. The tree trembled in the still air and sighed a deep, cold breath that pushed Morris onto his back.

Eve stood transfixed in the glow of the great pearl light. The impish lizard leaped into the tree and smiled as brightly as the leaves. Morris rolled onto his belly, sick with a nameless fear. Something was wrong. He felt it tingling in every nerve of his body as his brain shrieked an alarm. Where was God? Couldn't He see what was happening? Didn't He care? Eve stepped forward, entranced by the radiant light. The swaying lizard began to sing, its soft voice ringing like crystal. He was calling her. Morris put out his hand, summoning every ounce of his will not to run.

"No." His voice cracked just above a whisper. "No. No. No." There was nothing else he could say. He shook his head, reaching out his arms to her. "NO." She couldn't even hear him. He began to cry, the tears freezing on his cheeks. "No, Eve. No." Why couldn't she understand? It was the end of the world. "No," he whimpered.

She took a step closer and lifted a hand from her side.

"No!" he sobbed.

❖ ❖ ❖

There was a rushing inside his head like the whip of a giant catapult and a hard thump and pain. His room was semi-light. The alarm clock was shrieking beside him. His neck was killing him. He sat up in bed and squeezed his temples between his fists. His face stung. He wanted to yell but couldn't think of anything appropriate to say.

"No," he whispered, "no."

Chapter 8

Vern wrestled the neck of a squeaking balloon into a knot.

"Isn't Hattie's birthday on Monday?" he asked.

Morris bobbed an affirmative answer from behind a growing circle of canary yellow before he paused for a breath. "Doing this on a Friday gives yours truly the weekend to clean up if need be," he said. "Besides, this is a surprise party. We couldn't plan this shindig on the actual day. It would be too obvious."

Vern laughed and stretched out another balloon. "Oh, she'll be surprised all right."

Morris smiled stiffly and tugged at his balloon. *What did Vern mean by that?* Maybe the party wasn't such a great idea after all. No one knew how Hattie would react to the public revelation of her very private secret. *Too late now.*

"How did you find out when her birthday is, anyway?" the principal asked.

Morris squelched a smile at the thought of Sheri's reconnaissance work with the personnel files. She had finally told him the whole story of how she had knocked things off Bridget's desk and then hurriedly read Hattie's file while the flustered secretary bent over to retrieve them.

The next day Morris overheard Bridget in the teachers' lounge commenting to another secretary that Sheri Wallace had to be "the clumsiest creature God ever made."

"Let's just say it took some serious digging," Morris replied, picking up another balloon.

"Ahh," Vern said, "a good magician never reveals his secrets."

Morris stopped tying balloons to survey the gym, which was bustling with activity. Teachers on their lunch breaks strung pink and green streamers between the walls and scrawled out poster board signs. Pete teetered on a wooden ladder, making jokes about activating his workmen's comp while trying to adjust the height of the "Happy Birthday Miss Hattie" banner Morris had ordered from a local print shop.

Sheri had taken Hattie out to lunch.

"How long do we have until the eagle lands?" Vern queried, cackling to himself.

"Roger that, base camp," Morris replied. "The eagle is with the chickadee. Estimated time of arrival is thirty minutes."

"Thirty minutes," Vern muttered. "We better shift this decorating into overdrive."

Things were coming together: The gym looked appropriately festive, the chocolate sheet cake with its delicate yellow frosting flowers was boxed carefully in the refrigerator in the teachers' lounge, and the teachers who weren't decorating were gathering their classes together for a march down to the gym. Everything was going as planned.

Morris wandered into the hall and began to pace as he thought. It felt good to be at work, surrounded by rational coworkers and friends. As he looked around he saw one serene face after another, confident in the knowledge that the world, though not perfect, was a decent place after all. They didn't take piddling night terrors too seriously. They weren't checking for reptiles in every shadow, fearing for their lives with every bump in the dark. He inhaled deeply. He could almost smell the sanity.

Morris leaned back against the window, letting his black shirt sop up the scattered warmth of the sun. That was it. He was just taking his dreams too much to heart. Everyone had the occasional nightmare. Everyone woke up from time to time drenched in fearful sweat. Such things were ignored, and life went on. He would let his dreams run their course, and his subconscious would move on to irritatingly fixate on something else.

I can only hope. He wondered momentarily what Hattie would think of his dreams. She was usually the first person he went to for advice on everything from women to work to money, but his dreams were . . . different, to say the least. They were just too personal. *Maybe I just don't want to admit that I've been spooked.* He shivered at the memory of the glistening tree. Besides, he knew what Hattie would say. Hattie, who hadn't missed a Sunday at church since the day she was born, whose rear end had undoubtedly worn a groove in her favorite pew by now, who quoted Scripture verbatim, with gusto, whenever an opportunity arose. For once, the last thing he wanted to hear was Hattie's point of view.

Doors opened down the hall, swinging silently on the hinges he kept oiled. The kids treaded lightly in somewhat orderly rows, and he didn't have to look at their faces to know they were bubbling inside. Some of them clutched presents at their sides, small projects made in art class and pictures drawn for the jubilant event. It was a minor miracle the secret of the party had been kept for so long.

Sophie cruised by with her class, herded into place by another teacher during Sheri's brief absence. She wore an impossibly wide but quiet grin that showcased her missing teeth. Just as Morris stretched out his hand to give one of her long braids a tug, Vern rushed in from the parking lot.

"The eagle has landed! The eagle has landed!" he yelled. "Get everyone into the gym. I'll get the cake."

There was a flurry of frantic activity as the last few teachers squeezed their chattering kids into the gym. No one was quiet anymore. In the anticipation of the moment the invisible gag order was forgotten. Even the older kids, who understood the importance of silence, made the situation worse by wedging their forefingers against their lips and loudly shushing everyone else.

She'll hear this circus a mile away. Morris jumped onto a chair and waved his arms above his head. "Everyone quiet down!" he bellowed. "Be quiet. Beee quieeett." The squealing, hopping, pushing mass of children slowed to a milling crowd. When they were sufficiently still, he stepped off the chair.

"It's very important that we stay quiet," he continued, "so Miss Hattie won't hear us."

Suddenly they froze, eyes wide, hands popping up to mouths to suppress confused giggles.

"When Miss Wallace and Miss Hattie walk through the door behind me, I want you to yell 'surprise' as loud as you can. Okay?" A finger tapped his shoulder, but he ignored it.

"Morris!" Vern said urgently. "If I were you, I'd turn around."

A familiar voice sang into his left ear, "SURPRISE!"

He whirled around to find Hattie bent at the waist in a fit of laughter. Sheri did her best to pull a straight face, hiding her smile behind her shaking hands. Morris gaped for a second before he pulled it together.

"Look everyone!" he called over the tittering crowd. "It's Miss Hattie." He waved his fingers in the air like a conductor and broke into "Happy birthday to you, happy birthday to you . . ."

The kids and teachers loudly picked up the tune, but Vern just clutched his sides, a flow of helpless tears streaming down his pink face. For months to follow he could be reduced to a cackling heap with one word about Hattie's party and the look on Morris's face.

Hattie applauded as the off-key rendition wound down. She smiled broadly over the kids while shooting darts at a sheepish Morris with her eyes. Morris noticed with relief that she seemed genuinely touched when she saw the cake, and a few tears slipped from her eyes as the children came forward with their presents. She marveled over every drawing and card, kissed the beaming bearers soundly on the tops of their heads, and sent them scampering back to class. Sophie was the last one to crawl into her ample lap, toting a small purple box. As Hattie unwound the ribbon, Sophie explained something that Morris couldn't hear. Hattie's mouth suddenly quivered, and all hope of composure melted as her eyes flushed with tears. She gripped the little girl in a bear hug against her chest. When Sophie had gone skipping back to class at Sheri's side, Hattie sidled up to Morris, who was helping Pete stack the folding chairs back into the closet.

"I won't ask how you found out," she said, "because I probably don't want to know. But I will thank you." She blushed, and he realized that he had never seen her blush before. "I never thought I could enjoy a birthday party half as much as I did this one."

Morris threw his arm around her shoulder. "Believe me," he said, "it was our pleasure. It was especially Vern's pleasure."

She laughed at that.

"Hey, what did Sophie give you?" he asked.

She opened the box to reveal a small, gold-colored ring nestled against a fuzzy white background. A bit of glass twinkled from the middle of it.

"This cost her four dollars," Hattie explained as the tears began to flow again. "When you announced the party last week, she started doing extra chores around the house to earn the money. She even helped her neighbors sweep their steps and took out their trash." She wiped her cheeks with the back of her hand and straightened her shoulders. "This is now the most precious piece of jewelry I own."

Morris nodded and forced the rising cannonball back down his throat. "She is a treasure."

Hattie blotted at her eyes with a handkerchief and smoothed her hair with her hands. "Well, I guess it's time for me to get back to class. I'm glad you're the one in charge of cleanup, not me. There's a lot to throw away." She surveyed the fluttering streamers and the sea of balloons drifting back and forth across the floor. "But if you could," she said quietly, with a smile, "save that banner for me?"

Morris made quick work of the gym, procuring a safety pin from Vern's secretary to dispose of the balloons. He dragged the doors shut and went after the decorations with a vengeance, plucking the signs from the walls and mercilessly popping and trashing the dozens of rubber shells. He was far from sentimental, but tearing down the decorations felt wrong somehow, like the interruption of something important.

Is this how we celebrate a life like Hattie's? We set aside an hour of our time to drape plastic around a room and stuff our faces with cake? It was enough to depress anyone, even a cheerful guy like himself. He hoped she knew how much she meant to all of them. That was all that really mattered.

Nothing lasts forever. He yanked a fluttering streamer from the ceiling, then pulled down the prized banner and folded it into a manageable square before leaving it in the office for Hattie. What would she do with it? File it away in a drawer so it could be pulled out from time to time and reminisced over? Hang it over her couch for visitors to see? Maybe she'd just keep it as indisputable evidence that she had, at one time or another, celebrated her birthday. In the office, he gave Bridget his most charming smile.

"Sheri told me to tell you hello," he said.

❖ ❖ ❖

It was already one o'clock, and the fresh air of the playground was beckoning. Recess had been bumped back from its usual time to accommodate the party, and Morris could hear kids scurrying across the yard as he tied the last trash bag shut. He trotted outside to stretch his legs and look around. The kickball field was finally open for business again, much to the delight of Connor and James, who chased after the ball and each other with renewed fervor. Vern's police connection had searched the field and even checked the needle for fingerprints, to no avail. Apparently the addict who was careless enough to leave his or her drug paraphernalia on the school playground happened to be wearing gloves while shooting up.

"It's not that uncommon anymore," Detective McCloski explained to the teachers in the lounge one morning. "These sickos don't care about anyone but themselves. They don't care if they're endangering children or spreading incurable diseases as long as they get their fix and they don't get caught." He brushed the remnants of a powdered doughnut from his mustache and sighed as if he were about to reveal a shameful secret. "We're dealing with a smarter and more heartless breed of criminal than ever before," he said. "Sometimes it feels like a losing battle."

Morris looked toward the field, where a long-awaited rematch was taking place. Even from a distance he could see James Bakersfield's coppery hair bobbing around the bases as he dashed toward third. A plume of dirt spurted into the air as he slid face first into the plate. Morris wondered if there was another ten-year-old in the entire world who loved kickball as much as James.

He was halfway across the yard when he spotted Sheri pushing happy kindergarteners on the swings. Ah, that was a worthy diversion if ever there was one.

"Hey, you!" he called, crunching up beside her. "We actually pulled it off."

She gave an eager little girl one last push and turned toward him with a sly smile and extended hand. "I must say we make excellent partners in crime."

He shook the offered hand and covered it with his other one, unwilling to let go. Her fingers were cold. He wanted to press her cool palm flat against his chest and keep it there for a while but reminded himself that they were surrounded by curious little eyes.

"That was definitely a party for the record books," she said absently and slipped her hand into her pocket.

Does she object to holding my hand? Or does she know, like me, that a recess romance isn't a good idea? Did she put her hand in her pocket as a measure of self-control or self-

protection? Am I totally overanalyzing this? After all, she is coming over for dinner on Saturday.

The silence between them was palpable.

"Morris!" It was James, running their way with the kick-ball in his arms. "Are you coming or what?"

Morris waved him off. "Yeah, I'm coming, James. Just give me a sec." He couldn't leave Sheri with that faint friction rubbing silently between them.

"It was a fabulous idea, and I know it meant a lot to Hattie. We'll have to do this again next year."

"We will most definitely have to do this again next year," she replied.

He backed away and started for the field, grinning, as usual, like an idiot. Sheri's radiant smile warmed him from the inside out and drove from his mind any lingering clouds. Even the chill panic of his most recent dream seemed to melt in her presence.

Life could only be good with a woman like that by my side.

A sound from the street stopped his progress. He turned to face the road that ran by the school and felt again the approaching rumble, terribly deep. *It's just a car. Some yuppie on his cell phone in his mammoth SUV.*

Something didn't feel right. He looked around. Kids were chasing each other, laughing and playing as usual. Teachers chatted in clusters while keeping an eye on the kids. No one had fallen, no one was fighting, and no one was hurt. Why did that sound fill him with such unearthly dread? The eerie ringing of the serpent's song sounded in his memory. Morris shook off a crawling fear.

Stop it. He took a few steps closer to the busy street. Through the chain-link fence he saw cars whipping along, oblivious to the reduced speed limit of the school zone. He felt the rumble again, closer than before. An expensive car, sleek and dark, purred into view, and he wondered what torture the driver had put it through to make it sound like that.

It slowed to a crawl as it passed the school, inky windows reflecting the thin April sunlight. He suddenly remembered an article in the paper the week before profiling wealthy pedophiles that targeted school playgrounds for prey but firmly dismissed the idea. *That would never happen here.* Something clawed a warning in his gut.

It's just a car. He peered at the car, straining to make out the details of its year and model. One of the back windows slid open a crack, but its occupants stayed hidden in the shadows.

It's nothing. A glint of flinty gray caught his eye as he turned away. The sunlight bounced off something protruding from the depths of the car. He squinted.

That isn't . . . it can't be. The reality of the gun didn't hit home until the first bullet whizzed by his ear. Another pinged off the slide. The teachers looked up, startled by the sound.

What's happening? Is someone shooting? at children?

The confusion was immobilizing. It wasn't possible. No one shot at children like that. There was another pop, then a sickening splash and a scream. One of the teachers crumpled to the ground, gripping her bleeding hand.

"Get down! Get down!" Morris screamed. He crashed into the hopscotch game next to him and tackled the children to the ground.

"Stay down," he whispered urgently as the girls began to cry. It was all happening so fast. *Ping. Ping.* Bullets bounced off the pavement. He pounced on the swings and dragged the kids into the gravel, pressed Sheri's head firmly to the pavement.

"Keep them down!" he yelled as a spray of bullets bounced around them. He crawled over to the jungle gym where a dozen kids hung frozen in fear. "Down!" he yelled. "Get down."

He grabbed at the tangle of shirts and legs. A bullet ricocheted off the monkey bars. He pulled down armfuls of kids and dragged them through the dirt to the slide where he stuffed them underneath and lay across them. Bullets hailed through the metal chutes, and the children screamed. He shielded them as best he could. Someone was moaning softly above them.

Morris poked his head out. Connor Parker was stuck on the slide. "Connor, c'mon!" he screamed at the quaking boy.

Connor shook his head and plastered himself flat against the slide. A bullet hit the wooden crossbar above his head with a dull thud, and he started to cry. The children sobbed.

Morris pried himself free of their clinging hands, wriggled out from his hiding place, and leaped into the air. He grabbed Connor in one smooth motion as he rolled across the slide. They tumbled to the ground, and try as he might, Morris couldn't help landing on Connor's arm as they hit the earth. There was a crunch like the splintering of wood, and Connor cried out in pain.

The bullets stopped. For a moment all was silent.

Morris popped his head up to look around. Thank God the kickball field was out of range of the bullets. Thank God those teachers had quick reflexes. Clusters of sobbing children lay prone all over the blacktop; frightened teachers had flung their bodies over the mounds of kids. He didn't see any blood.

The earthy rumble sounded again as the gun retracted and the car pulled away. As he watched it purr back into the street, something inside him came unhinged. His muscles began to move of their own free will. There was an engine roaring in his ears, revving higher and higher until it screamed like his steaming teakettle. His vision wobbled, and the car bounced before his eyes.

Is this rage? He sprang up and let forth a stream of profanity.

What am I doing? He sprinted after the retreating car like a madman. Lactic acid burned in his frenzied legs as they gobbled up the space separating him from the gun-toting gangsters. Someone screamed at him in a freakish voice.

"Kill you! I'll . . . kill . . . you . . . all! I'm killing you!"

He was within twenty yards of the car, pumping his arms and legs until he thought his heart would burst, when the driver punched the gas. Morris grabbed a rock and flung it with all his might at the vanishing vehicle. It smacked the rear window with a resounding crack, and a loud curse issued from within. He fell to his knees, panting like an animal. There was blood on his pants.

This isn't happening. Isn't happening. Not in my school. Not to us. Not to us. Not to us. He gasped for a breath.

Nothing lasts forever.

Chapter 9

Paper crinkled thinly around his ears. The fresh sheets stretched out over the cot in the small school infirmary smelled pleasantly untouched. Morris turned over with a groan and buried his face in them. His mouth was awash in the chalky residue of half a dozen hastily chomped antacid tablets. He ran his tongue over his teeth and picked stray bits from his molars.

"How are you feeling, Morris?" Lynn's normally gruff voice was marked with such tenderness that he almost didn't recognize it. As the school's only nurse for the past fifteen years, she had finely tuned her abilities to sort real emergencies from exaggerated ailments and showed scant mercy to any little con artist gutsy enough to test her.

He pulled himself into a seated position with his back against the wall and immediately regretted it. Acid churned in his abdomen, nipping viciously at his empty stomach. He bit his lip and gave her a halfhearted grin, but he knew his face belied him.

She raised her eyebrows and wrinkled her nose. "That bad, huh?" She wrapped her long, graying hair into a bun at the back of her neck and jabbed it firmly into place with a pencil. "I wish I had something stronger to give you, honey, but I don't. Try drinking some more water."

He shook his head. "Thanks, Lynn, but I'll be all right."

She sat down next to him, flattening a length of paper and sending a whoosh of air from the tired cot. From the way she looked him over, he could tell she was about to broach a delicate subject.

"It's not your stomach I'm worried about, Morris." She paused, hoping for an interruption, but he had nothing to say. "You really went berserk out there. I know it was pretty traumatic." She tapped her forefinger against her temple. "Are you going to be okay here?"

Morris chewed on his lip. *How am I supposed to answer that? No? I'm certifiable? Commit me now?*

"I said some pretty awful stuff in front of the kids, didn't I?" he asked.

"It's not that big of a deal." She laughed, but it sounded forced. "I'm sure they hear worse at home."

Sure, if their parents are sailors. He didn't want to ask, but he had to know. "Lynn . . . what else did I do?"

"You don't remember?" She furrowed her brow.

"I vaguely recall throwing a rock at the car." He shook his head. "I feel like I'm losing my mind."

"No." She pulled out the corner of her shirt to attack a spot on the glasses that hung from her neck on a chain. "Short-term memory loss is common in true fits of rage and episodes of trauma. Years ago, when I was doing my rounds as a student nurse, I saw a lot of that, what with Vietnam and all." She hesitated. "After you threw the rock you had to be restrained."

"What?" He jumped off the sofa and walked the length of the small office in two steps. "Please tell me you're kidding." *I'm not a violent person.*

"It took Pete and Vern and a couple of cops to settle you down."

He rubbed the back of his neck; he could tell she was holding back. "What else?"

"You gave Pete an awful shiner." She closed her eyes as she said it, as if she couldn't bear to see his face.

"I hit Pete?" He wanted to cry.

She nodded miserably and helped him back to the cot. "I told you," she said carefully, "you really lost it."

He was silent.

"Hey," she continued in an artificially cheery voice, "we have to be thankful. It's a miracle no one was seriously hurt. It was horrible, but it's over now."

A knock on the door stalled her pep talk, and Morris couldn't help but think that she looked relieved. It was Detective McCloski, looking every bit the part in his belted tan overcoat and hat. Morris wanted to ask him if the outfit was standard issue in detective school or if he had to mail away for it separately but refrained. McCloski took off his hat and set it on Lynn's cluttered desk.

"How are you feeling, Morris?"

That seems to be the question of the day. He smiled weakly. "I've been better."

McCloski spotted the empty bottle of antacids. "Your stomach's waging war on you, huh?" He pulled a chair around to face the cot and sat down. "May I ask you a few questions?"

Morris nodded. *Do I have a choice?* "Of course."

"Okay," he said, jumping right in. "First, let me assure you that the threats you made against the shooters will not be recorded as evidence. I've made sure of that. Anyone would have said the same."

Morris shot Lynn a questioning look, but she was conveniently sorting packages of cotton balls with her back turned to him.

"I made threats?" he asked numbly.

"Well, you threatened to kill them." He consulted his notepad matter-of-factly. "Your exact words were 'kill you all, I'll kill you all. . . .'"

"Enough." Morris pinched the bridge of his nose. "I get the picture."

The detective switched topics. "Did you happen to note the make, model, year, or license plate of the car?"

What was that in his voice? It seemed rougher than before. What was he insinuating? The walls leaned in on Morris. The hanging light above them began to sway. Lynn's office, once a refuge for the sick, was suddenly a hostile place. His temples pulsed, and he wondered if they were visibly bulging out from the sides of his head.

Think, Morris. What did you see? Numbers flashed in his vision; the back of the car and a silver frame zipping away. "Five, eight, six. The last three digits of the license plate were five, eight, six."

"You sure?" McCloski asked.

"I'm positive." *Sorry, I was too busy pitching rocks and screaming like a lunatic to read the entire plate or do anything remotely useful.* He sensed too late the edge in his voice and started to apologize.

"Hey, don't worry about it," the detective interrupted.

"You did the best you could. From what I hear you saved a lot of lives." He flipped the notebook shut and leaned back in the chair. "Especially that Parker kid. Man, he'd be dead if it weren't for you."

Morris felt himself falling through space. He saw the gravel and the ground rushing up to meet him and Connor's small arm twisting beneath his body as he felt the rub of the fragile bones. It was too much. He grabbed the trash can from under Lynn's desk and wretched. When he pulled his head out, his throat was raw, his eyes were streaming, and Detective McCloski had a strange expression on his face. Was it sympathy? pity? disgust?

"Hey, Morris, why don't you go home and get some rest? There are just a few more questions. We can go over them later."

He nodded and stumbled up from the cot, pushing away the glass of water Lynn offered.

❖ ❖ ❖

Morris wandered through the halls, unnerved by the gaping silence that laughing, pushing children should have filled. All after-school activities had been canceled, and frightened parents had rushed from work to snatch their children from the gnashing jaws of death while he had been occupied with Lynn. In a way, he was glad he had missed them. He couldn't have borne the panic, the horror he would have seen in their eyes.

He looked out the window at the playground, corralled in police barricades and strung with fluttering crime-scene tape. Forensic experts sifted through the gravel and grass like nervous hens, scratching the earth for any clue. One whipped out a pair of oversized tweezers and wrenched at a bullet imbedded in the wooden post of the swing set. He dropped it into a baggie, a satisfied look on his face. TV news trucks were lined up outside the fence, and reporters gazed longingly past the barricades at the breaking story as they primped for the cameras.

Morris pressed gingerly against the hollow beneath his ribs. The inferno was flaring. He had to get out of there. He rounded the corner at the entrance to the school and crashed full speed into Hattie, whose nose met his sternum at an alarming speed.

"Hattie!" He gripped her beneath her elbows as she regained her balance. "Are you all right?"

She nodded and squeezed her nose tenderly. Two huge tears rolled over it. "I'm fine," she said, then looked him over and burst into tears.

He reached his arm around her as she sobbed into his shoulder.

"Oh, Morris," she wailed. "Thank God you're okay." She pulled a handkerchief from the pocket of her blazer to dab at her eyes. "Sorry about that." She smiled a sad little smile and straightened his rumpled shirt. "I'm okay now."

"Hattie," he pleaded, "get me out of here. Another minute in this place and I'll be vomiting molten lava."

She hesitated. "Vern wanted to see you, but that can wait until Monday, I suppose. How about I walk you home?" She took his arm and steered him down the hall. "It's not that far, and the fresh air will do you good."

He nodded. It was a good mile and a half to his apartment on foot. If he had been thinking clearly, he never would have let her walk that far, but all he could think of were the bullets and the crying children and Connor's tiny body crumpling beneath his.

Hattie was talking as they approached the doors. He stopped her. "I'm sorry, Hattie. What were you saying?"

"I was saying that there are a lot of people out there who want to talk to you."

"To me?" He couldn't hide his chagrin.

"You're the hero, honey, and everybody loves a hero." They paused at the doors. Outside he could see the throng of people on the sidewalk with their cameras ready and their tape recorders poised.

"Oh, Lord . . ." Hattie murmured.

"I didn't know there were so many reporters in the city," he said.

"It's a big city."

He hesitated. "McCloski told me not to tell them too much."

She reached up and patted his cheek. "Then don't tell them anything."

He took a deep breath, squared his shoulders, and opened the door. *Here goes.*

The mass of chattering reporters turned as one body, and he was instantly surrounded. Cameras clicked and whirred and flashed and clicked, and microphones hovered under his chin. The questions flew from everywhere.

"Morris, are you hurt?"

"Do you plan to press charges if the shooters are caught?"

"Did you see the suspects?"

"Tell us what happened."

He grasped Hattie's hand and waded through the crowd, towing her protectively behind him. He was getting his fifteen minutes of fame, that was for sure.

"What's the name of the little boy who broke his arm?"

"Mr. Jackson, how do you feel?"

He stopped and lifted his bowed head. They closed in around him. Hattie pushed at his back to urge him on.

"How do you feel?" the voice asked again.

His lungs burned. His fists ached with longing. Pain shot through his jaw as he ground his teeth together. *How do I feel?* He looked over their heads toward the playground. Cameras flashed.

"Angry," he growled and pushed his way past.

He flew up the street, his arms flailing and his eyes burning with an anger that wouldn't translate into tears. Kids on bikes and perusing patrons of a nearby newsstand scattered out of the way as he passed. Gruesome visions clotted in his mind: bleeding children, dying teachers, a bullet-ridden Sheri gasping her final breath. He drove on, flinging a pair of trash cans from his path.

Hattie bustled along at his side, her mincing steps barely keeping up. "Dear, can you slow down? I can't compete with those long legs of yours." Her skin was bright with perspiration, and she was puffing for air.

Morris immediately checked his pace. "I'm sorry," he said. "My mind is somewhere else."

"That's better," she panted as they slowed to a walk. He couldn't help but notice that she moved with surprising agility for someone on the plumper side of life. It was almost enough to make him smile.

They continued on in silence for a block, then two. The streets grew narrower and the trees scarcer as they wove their way through shabby tenements and alleys that ran behind mom-and-pop grocery stores and pharmacies. Elderly women leaned from curtained windows to drape their damp laundry over sunny fire escapes.

He winced at the sight of dozens of children playing in the streets. *How many of them won't live long enough to grow into men and women?* He watched them running and laughing, their balls and bikes and sticks steered by happy hands. No worry clouded their faces, no fear. They knew nothing of sorrow yet, nothing of loss, but they would learn. It was only a matter of time.

A door opened, and a woman stepped out onto the cement with her hand on her hip. She called her son in from the frolicking herd with a voice that prevented any dawdling on his part. He dragged his feet reluctantly inside, and as Morris watched them he wondered which was worse: to lose a loved one by sheer accident or at the deliberate hands of someone else.

If any of the children had died that afternoon, it would have been tragic, but at least there would be someone to blame. There would be an investigation, a manhunt, a trial, a sentence. Some obscene excuse for a human being would stand before the jury and cry about how his parents never loved him and how their coldness made him trigger-happy, and it would be unacceptable, but it would be a reason. There would be justice. There would be some sense of closure.

But what about his loss? What about his father? There was no sense, no logic to it. No explanation but a moving car, an icy road, a faulty seat belt. No justice and no one to blame, except maybe Morris himself. He sent his father to his death. The thoughtlessness of a ten-year-old took his mother's husband away. *It can't be my fault. I can't live with that.*

Hattie was humming something vaguely familiar with the soothing presence of a forgotten time and place. The rich notes filled her whole frame and reverberated in his ears.

"What is that?" His voice sounded dry. "It's familiar."

She reached out a hand and rubbed the middle of his back.

"It's an old, old hymn, dear," she replied, tracing circles between his shoulder blades. "It speaks of the perfect mercy of God."

He stiffened. *I must be thinking of a different God. The God I know knocks off helpless children at play. He sends earthquakes and famines and plagues, for what? To weed us out? Thin down the population a little? What, are there too many of us to keep track of? God, who killed my father; who let me take the blame for it. Oh, the infinite mercy of God. Who demands a level of perfection that no one can meet, then punishes us for it. Oh, God! Please, no more of Your perfect mercy!*

"Morris!" Hattie clutched at his arm. What was wrong with her? Her voice was so tight. She let out a stifled whimper as he turned to face her.

"What?" he whispered. He looked around. Did someone have a gun? Was there a robbery in progress behind them?

"Morris," she hissed, "what's wrong?" She was trembling. "Your face. I've never seen you look so angry. Like you want to hurt someone."

My face? He touched his cheek and felt the iron plane of his jaw. A muscle beneath his right eye began to spasm.

"What's going on with you?" she asked.

He sank onto the bench of a nearby bus stop and kicked away the trash at his feet.

She sat down next to him, gripping the back of the bench nervously. "I understand that you're angry," she said. "I'm angry too. We all could have been killed. Our children could have been killed. And it's natural to feel hate toward the ones who did it . . ."

"It's not them." He unclenched his jaw and opened his eyes. The brick wall of the produce market across the street was scrawled with obscene graffiti in fuzzy strains of blue and black.

"What?"

"It's not the shooters that I'm angry with."

"Then who?"

"It's God." *Let's see how she handles that. Let's see what Hattie and her precious God think of me now.*

She was silent. He could still hear children playing somewhere, the dull ring of a basketball against the pavement, and farther off the roar of a city bus making its rounds. A caustic remark was making its way past his teeth when he felt her cool, soft hand on his face. Something wet squeezed from beneath his eyelid. She cradled his jaw with a motherly touch and stroked at the corner of his eye with her thumb.

"I'm so sorry," she whispered. "I want so badly for you to know the God I know. To know what He did for us, and why the world is the way it is." She paused. "But I know that's not what you want to hear right now."

He squeezed her hand tightly.

"He loves you. That's all I can say."

If only I could believe that. There was a mystery in her words that soothed him. He figured it was the kindness of an old friend that held him in that brief pocket of bright hope.

The distant bus roared around the corner and bore down on them in a cloud of diesel fumes and a squeal of brakes. He dug a handful of change from his pocket.

"Hattie, I want you to get on this bus and go home." He pressed the money into her hand.

"Morris, I can't leave you now." She shook her head. "Not in this state. You're a wreck."

He was insistent. "I'll call you when I get home to let you know I'm all right. Now go!" The bus wheezed up to the curb, and he turned her around and marched her toward the open door.

"I'll be waiting by the phone," she said. "Don't let an old woman worry, Morris!"

He waved and watched the bus lurch away into the fading afternoon. At last, again, he was alone.

Chapter 10

Morris opened his eyes. Four cracked white walls enclosed him. A sloping ceiling met them in seamless curves above his head. Nothing moved. He knew exactly where he was.

"It's Saturday," he murmured as he stretched his arms and pedaled his legs in circles beneath the sheets. "I'm at home, in my own room, in my own bed." He sat up and ground his fists into his eyes until they watered. *Just another day to survive.*

What had happened to him? Somewhere in the dim slush of spring, his life had become nothing more than a series of disoriented wakings. He didn't want to think about it. He pulled a shirt over his head and staggered out to the kitchen, swinging his arms like windmill blades to loosen his stiff shoulders.

Ouch. His forearm tugged painfully. He brought his arm around and noticed for the first time the ugly gash scrawled from his wrist bone halfway to his elbow. It was deep, but it wasn't oozing. He poked at the scab that sutured the two sides of the gaping wound together. *What else did I do to myself?* He ran his hands along his torso, patting suspiciously here and there. *Nothing broken.* There was a long, speckled scrape along his ribs and a series of misshapen bruises on his legs.

"No one ever said being a superhero was easy," he muttered and reached for a cereal bowl. A red light blinked from the kitchen counter. He groaned.

My poor mother. How could I forget to call?

He tapped the scolding red eye and waited for her voice to fill the room. She breathed heavily, and he could tell she was pinching off the tears between breaths.

"Morris, I heard about the shooting on the news. Are you all right? Please call me as soon as you get this, darling, *please.*" There was a pause. A muffled sob. "We've got to know that you're okay."

He grabbed his phone from its mount on the wall and punched in the numbers. It rang twice before William's quiet voice answered.

"Hello?"

Hello, Dad. The word was on his lips. He caught himself. *My father is dead.* There was a moment of confused silence.

"Hello?"

"William!" He stuttered, "It . . . it's Morris. I'm fine. I'm sorry . . ."

"Oh, thank God!" Was William about to cry? "Sandra! It's Morris. He's okay."

"Morris!" She was crying. "Are you all right? They said on the news that someone was shot through the hand."

"That was one of the teachers."

". . . And someone else broke an arm."

"That was one of the students."

"So you're unhurt?" William asked.

Morris ran his hand along his side. "Just a few scrapes and bruises," he said. "Minor stuff."

"Thank You, Jesus," William sighed.

"We must have tried calling ten times last night, but you never answered." Sandra's voice was unbearably thick.

"I'm so sorry, Mom." *Words can't express.* "I was at school late talking to the police, and by the time I got home I had just enough energy to collapse and pull the door shut behind me. Honestly, I didn't check my messages until just now."

"It's all right," she soothed, "as long as you're okay." A moment of silence passed, a fraction of a heartbeat.

"How are you holding up, honey? It must have been awful."

"I'm—" *enraged . . . frightened . . . bitter . . . losing touch with reality* "—okay, Mom. I'm okay."

"Why don't you come stay with us for a while? I hate to think of you alone in that apartment."

The idea was strangely appealing. Visions of warmth and laughter and light pressed on his senses. *What am I thinking? I'm a grown man.*

"No, Mom, really, I'm okay," he said. "I'm fine, but what if I stop by today? Maybe this afternoon?"

"We'd love that, Morris," William said. "We'll be waiting."

"Morris." It was Sandra again. "Please," she pleaded, "let me pray for you here on the phone."

He squirmed. Out of sheer habit he closed his eyes and listened to the cadence of her voice as she petitioned God on his behalf. It was like eavesdropping on a conversation in which he was the topic.

"And fill him with the peace of Jesus," she concluded. "In Jesus' name, Amen."

He clicked off and waited expectantly for the overwhelming influx of peace. Nope, it wasn't working.

There was a second message on the machine, this one from Sheri: calming yet hesitant and ever mindful of his fragile mental state. He writhed inside. What kind of a fool had he made of himself in front of her?

"Listen, I'll completely understand if you want a rain check on tomorrow night. We can always do dinner another time. On the other hand, I'd love to spend some time with you if you're up to it. If I don't hear from you, I'll just assume we're still on, and I'll see you then."

He played the message again. She sounded so relaxed. That had to be a good sign. She couldn't think he was too maniacal if she'd spend an evening alone with him. He picked up the phone and started to dial her number, then changed his mind. He had to make her understand, but what could he tell her? *Should I apologize?* Maybe by tonight he would know what to say.

He gulped down the soupy Cheerios at the bottom of the bowl and looked at the clock. It was after ten. The game was just starting, and Congo was undoubtedly talking trash about him in his absence. *I can't go. I can hardly walk straight, let alone hold a basketball.*

He looked around. The sterile white walls turned the sunlight cold, and the longer he sat there, the more institutional the room began to feel. Why hadn't he ever decorated? He supposed it was because he didn't have the money to buy anything worth hanging up. In the emptiness, his mind wandered back to the day before. Screams echoed sharply in the empty room. He closed his eyes and saw a pile of children huddled beneath him, their pupils dilated in the shadows beneath the slide. Little hands clung to him, and frightened voices wailed for moms and dads. *It's over. It's over.*

Without warning, a loud pop rang from the street below, followed by a hollow bursting sound. He fell over his own tangled feet as he dived to the window and slammed his ribs into the sill. The street was silent. No bodies lay strewn on the sidewalk, no bleeding children were curled on the asphalt. There was nothing but an ancient Cadillac sputtering away, a blue cloud hanging over its tailpipe. His heart pounded in his chest, and he knew that he had to get out of there.

❖ ❖ ❖

Fractured as he felt, Morris couldn't help but revel just a little in the glorious morning walk to the courts. The sun was blazing full force and hinting at the summer to come, while trees and grass were sporting the signature brassy green of spring, and buttery daffodils burst from their paper sheaths in the occasional tended yard. A few hardy birds twittered over all. It was almost enough to drive the horror of Friday from his mind, but even as he turned his face to the slicing breeze, he couldn't shake a lingering sadness.

Why is beauty never without pain? Can't one exist without the other? He dribbled his basketball nervously as he loped along, enjoying the stinging smack of the rubber against the street. *Why am I thinking about this anyway? I need a vacation.*

The sounds of the game reached his ears before the crowded courts came into view. Marrow-jolting music pounded from someone's stereo. Nasal female voices jeered unintelligibly above the dull thud of bodies slamming together and the ping of the basketball against the blacktop. Congo had brought his friends, as promised. Three or four of them crowded beneath the basket as Congo went up for a dunk. He missed, as usual, and Morris winced as his buddies fumbled sluggishly for the rebound. *Enough of this tortured soul bit. I'm going to play some ball.*

"Morris!" A heavyset girl on the sidelines called and waved. She turned her head to the game in progress. "Hey, C! Your competition's here!"

Darn. He could never remember her name. *Jen? Janet? Juanita?* It was a shame. She seemed the most intelligent of the girls who regularly attended the games. *When in doubt, improvise.* "Hey, J!" He waved. "You're looking lovely today."

She beamed, and Congo jogged toward him, winded and dripping with sweat.

"Didn't think you'd show," he panted, grabbing the ball from Morris and cradling it against his chest. "Thought maybe you were 'fraid."

"Of what?" Morris taunted. "That sorry bunch of friends you brought?"

Congo chucked the ball at his head in disgust. "You don't know what you're in for, boy."

"Show me. "

Congo looked up into his eyes. "Let's play," he grunted.

"Sure you don't need to rest?" Morris asked. "You look a little tired."

"Never," Congo said.

Morris shrugged and tossed his shirt into the pile near the staring girls.

"We're goin' two-on-two," Congo said. "You play with Beady." He motioned to a lumbering youth who was several inches shorter than Morris but twice as wide.

Beady? He looked his stocky new partner over. *It's got to be those shifty eyes.*

"All right, Beady," he said, grabbing the ball. "Let's whip these fools."

Beady grunted his approval, then promptly dropped the first pass Morris sent his way. It became quickly and painfully obvious to Morris why Congo had paired him with Beady: The poor guy was all brawn but no skill. Congo's exaggerated snickering at every brick Beady lobbed into the air became almost unbearable.

Even so, Morris was in fine form. The heat of the asphalt rose to soothe his tired muscles while the ball rolled easily from his fingers, arching perfectly with every shot. He leaped and bent and stretched and lunged without pause while the sultry smell of the sun and the tar, the salt and the sweat and the growing grass hung around him like sweet perfume. Congo never had a chance. Halfway through the game Morris knew that he would win and knew just as surely that Congo wouldn't ask for a rematch.

An hour later Beady was beaming. The sun bounced blindingly off the knobs on his shaved head as he hopped around the court crowing as though he owned a large slice of the world. The girls on the sidelines bobbed their heads knowingly from side to side.

"As if he had anything to do with that game," one commented to her neighbor. "He might as well have been sitting here with us."

The other girl laughed and hiked her already short skirt up a little higher as Morris walked by.

"Oh, girl, he'll never notice you," her girlfriend clucked.

Morris smiled to himself and made a beeline to his crumpled shirt. The girl whose name he could never remember offered him a bottle of water, which he happily tore open and emptied over his head. Cold rivulets streamed down his face and over his lips as he mopped his brow. It was shaping up to be a great day.

"Girl, look at that." A young lady at his feet latched onto her friend with a whisper. "Congo's gettin' into it with Vice."

"Today was my day!" Congo ranted, thrusting his stubby finger at his partner as his voice grew embarrassingly shrill. "You know how long I've been waitin' to beat that punk?"

"If you had made some of those shots, we could have," Vice replied, an inch from Congo's nose. "Your girl could've played a better game."

Congo's girl was thrusting her hips and wagging her fingers up and down the length of the court. "Don't be talkin' about me or my man that way," she muttered to no one in particular.

Congo snarled, "You're scared, man. I know you're thinkin' about that drive-by yesterday. You can't focus. You're thinkin' you might have killed some kid, and now you're worried you'll get caught."

Vice laid the flat of his hand on Congo's chest and pushed. "Fool," he spat. "You don't know what you're talkin' about."

Congo flailed back two steps before he caught himself. His girlfriend stopped her muttering long enough to look worried as the air grew thick around them.

Congo bounced back into Vice, jutting out his chest. "I do know that you hit a school." He paused for an instant to suck on the words. "The cops hear one word about it and they'll put you away. I don't care what gang you're bangin' for."

Vice slung the first punch too wide, and Congo dodged it with ease. He cocked his right arm to return the blow but never got the chance. Morris was already there.

He was enjoying the spat from the sidelines and warding off the unwelcome advances of some of the bolder girls. Beady was strutting back and forth like a rooster over his hens, laughing and pointing and expressing what Morris felt every week but was too good of a sport to ever show. He had been in the middle of a polite but firm refusal when the words "drive-by" found their way into the morning air.

His arms went limp. He stopped fighting the girls and strained to hear. *Drive-by?* His forearm flamed, the bruises on his legs ached. His ears rang with the whine of passing bullets. Before he knew what he was doing, he was halfway across the court. He stopped. Some shred of common sense was pleading its case.

There are dozens of shootings in this city every day. Hundreds, probably. You don't know that he's talking about the one at Quiley Heights. The guy deserved a beating just for being in a gang, but Morris knew he wasn't the one to give it. He cursed his nagging conscience and turned to walk away but found that he couldn't move. A devilish hiss, pushed through Congo's lips, lunged at the back of his head, and the hot stench of his nightmares billowed around his neck.

Where is it? His skin crawled. *Is it here?* Words garbled like a warped recording from Congo's mouth: hit . . . school . . . gang . . . Morris turned, and there before him stood the wreckage of the beast in human form: the puller of the trigger, the driver of the shaded car.

Vice yelped in surprise as Morris crashed down upon him.

What am I doing? He felt a whistling in his lungs and saw his own fists moving without instruction. One punch burst the vessels around Vice's left eye while another drove his fleshy nose back into his face.

One . . . two . . . one . . . two . . . His fists fell into rhythm. *How does it feel to be shot at?* His hands were slick with blood, but still he pounded, seeing himself as from a distance. Vice's jaw crumpled like tinfoil, his glazed eyes rolled back into his skull as consciousness fled into merciful night, and still Morris pummeled. The face beneath him was a pulpy mess, but still he hit until his fists were too wet and too weak to hit anymore.

"How does it feel to be dead?" Morris yelled. He was crying. Crying and beating and banging Vice's head weakly against the pavement. Blood spread out in a rusty pool over the concrete. "This could have been their blood." He couldn't see. The world was red and bleary. "This could have been their blood . . . the children," he whimpered, finally spent. He lay down next to Vice, hovering on the edge of darkness. The concrete, the blood, and his tears were warm, and he felt sleepy. Out of nowhere came sirens and garish, flashing lights, rousing him as his face hit the ground.

"I killed it," he whispered. "We're safe now."

A stern voice barked commands he couldn't understand.

God?

Stern hands twisted his arms and dragged him across the ground. Cold metal clamped onto his wrists.

I killed it.

He was lifted into a car.

I killed it, Eve.

Chapter 11

The cop car sped from the courts and into the bustling streets. Morris rolled limply across the backseat as the car jolted along, roused by the sharp smells of plastic and grease and metal. The reality of where he was and what had happened came to him in pieces, and the fight, though fresh on his hands, seemed distant, an embarrassing incident from a forgotten past.

The police radio crackled with breaking news of crime all over the city. There was an armed robbery at a bakery up north, a possible vehicular homicide in Quiley Heights, and a domestic abuse call from the east side. Three different shootings were called in during the short ride to the station.

It's only twelve o'clock, Morris mused. *I thought gang bangers and murderers slept in.*

The officer in the passenger's seat grabbed the receiver.

"We're bringing in an aggravated assault from just south of Quiley Heights. Estimated time of arrival, five minutes."

Aggravated assault? I'm an aggravated assault? Morris craned his neck around to look at his shackled hands. They were covered with blood. A wide swatch of blood was smeared across the vinyl seat. There was blood drying beneath his nails. An image of Vice's disfigured face flashed before his eyes. *Oh, God!* Bile climbed his esophagus. *Oh, God! I'm a murderer. What have I done? But he deserved it. He tried to kill me. He tried to kill Sheri.* "Officer?" *Why is my voice so hoarse?* "Officer, what happened to Vice?"

The cop on the radio turned around, her mouth set in a grim line. "What?"

"May I ask what happened to Vice?"

"Who's Vice?" she snapped.

"The man I . . . uh . . . I assaulted." He choked on the word.

She turned to her partner. "Can you believe this guy?" she asked. "He wants to know what happened to the guy he just beat within an inch of his life."

I'm just another murderous thug to them.

She turned back around. "You broke his nose and his jaw, and you cracked open his skull. When we found you, you were crying and muttering something about children's blood. Happy now?" She looked as if she might spit in his direction.

He shivered. *I'm losing my mind.*

Suddenly she cocked her head to the side and gave him a look he didn't understand. "Ed," she asked her partner, "have we picked this guy up before?"

Ed shook his head. "Nah. His record's clean. Not even a parking ticket."

"That's strange," she mused. "He looks familiar."

"Listen," Morris slurred, "I've got to tell you something about that guy." *Why do my lips feel so fat?*

"What?"

"He's the one who did the drive-by on Quiley Heights Elementary yesterday. I'm sure you heard about that."

"We were there questioning witnesses afterwards," Ed said.

"I was there." Morris scooted to the edge of the seat. "I was on the playground when it happened. I talked to Detective McCloski afterwards."

Ed's partner clapped her hand over her mouth. "Are you Morris?" she asked.

He nodded.

"We heard all about you. You saved all those kids."

He shook his head. She was missing the point. "Vice is the one who did the drive-by," he mumbled.

She narrowed her eyes. "How do you know?

"There's a guy back at the courts who knows all about it," he insisted. "His name is Congo. You guys should talk to him. I don't know his real name." *I'm so tired.* He rested his head against the window as they pulled up to the station. A mangled face leered back at him in the faint reflection. The left side was raked with wide scratches and the forehead was caked with blood. A split and swollen lip would make smiling impossible for a while. *If my mother could see me now.*

Inside, the police station was a flurry of activity. An elderly couple waited in wooden chairs along the wall. The man clutched his cane and the woman her purse, and together they looked ready to fend off any hoodlums that came their way. Across the room, a couple of punks fidgeted under the gaze of an officer.

"We swear, man, that spray paint was for an art project,"

one pleaded as he shifted his weight from one foot to the other.

"Yeah, an art project for school," his friend chimed in.

"Mm-hmm." The cop scribbled on a notepad. "I found you two making an art project on the side of Mr. Wigham's store." He motioned to the old man, who shook his cane at the boys and muttered angrily. "Sorry, boys, I'm going to have to bust you for this one."

"Awww, mannn," the shorter of the two groaned. "My mom is gonna kill me."

"Only if Mr. Wigham doesn't get to you first, son," the officer said and led them away.

Nearby, a man in an expensive suit and tie paced the room with a cell phone at his ear. "It wasn't just a car, honey," he whined. "It was my new Corvette. It was my midlife crisis car."

A cluster of young men loitered around the receptionist's desk waiting for news of a friend. One of them flashed his fingers in a twisted symbol as Morris was led by.

Sorry, brother, I'm not one of your kind.

Ed and his partner marched him into a small room without windows. Ed motioned to a chair, and Morris sat down awkwardly.

"Okay, Morris," he said, "we need to book you, but first I'm going to see if McCloski's around so we can get some of this mess straightened out."

Morris nodded. His arms were starting to go numb.

Ed bent over and looked into his eyes. "You understand?" he asked.

"Yeah, I understand," Morris said. "This is all just a little unreal."

"Well, kid, when you try to kill a man with your bare hands, you tend to end up at the police station. That's usually how it works." He pulled the door shut behind him and left Morris alone with his thoughts.

What have I done? A metallic taste filled his mouth, and the scratches on his face burned like a fresh brand. *I'm as bad as Vice. I'm as bad as any of the scum in here. When did I become a monster?* Despite the warmth of the room, a shiver ran up his spine. It was the same crawling sense that he wasn't alone, the same irrational fear that plagued him in his dreams. He blinked, and the room seemed darker than before. *Is it here?* He whipped around in his seat. *It isn't real,* he told himself. *It isn't real.*

The door opened, and he leaped out of his chair.

It was Detective McCloski. "Morris. You okay?"

"Yeah." Morris caught his breath. "For a moment I thought you were someone else."

The detective sat down across from the empty chair. "Please . . . sit," he said. "Morris, we need to talk. After what happened today I don't think you can deny that you're having some serious emotional issues because of the shooting. You may be suffering from post-traumatic stress syndrome." He flipped through the contents of a manila folder. "Whatever the case, you need to find a way to deal with this."

"Did Ed tell you about Vice?" Morris interrupted. "About his involvement in the shooting?"

McCloski sighed. "Yes, he did. I sent him to pick up your friend Congo. If his testimony makes sense, I'll head over to the hospital for a little chat with Vice."

Morris unwound a notch.

"But, Morris," the detective continued, "I'm not in here to talk about the case. I'm here to talk about you. You've got to get some help."

Morris nodded compliantly. "I know."

"Officers Petrillo and Jones happened to be driving by and saw the altercation from a distance." McCloski shuffled the papers in front of him. "I have their report. Would you like to make a statement in your defense?"

Morris leaned back against the chair and considered the question. *How could I possibly defend my actions?* "No," he said.

McCloski made a note on one of the forms.

"Now for the good news, if you want to call it that. Due to the strange nature of this incident, my involvement with the case, and your recent trauma, we can let a lot slide. If Vice doesn't press charges, which I'm pretty sure he won't, you're off the hook. We do have to book you, though, for administrative purposes."

Morris didn't like the sound of that. "What does that involve?"

"Fingerprinting, mug shots, a background check . . . the usual."

Morris set his head on the table. *This is going to kill my mother. Maybe I don't have to tell her.*

"Oh, and someone has to come pick you up. There's no way I'm letting you walk out of here on your own in this condition."

"Thanks, detective," Morris said. "I can't thank you enough. Now I've just got to figure out who to call."

McCloski cleared his throat. "Actually, I've already taken care of that." He smiled sheepishly. "I, uh, I called Hattie for you."

"Oh, noooo, " Morris groaned.

McCloski helped him out of his chair. "Let's take you out of these cuffs and get you washed up. The sooner we get this over with, the sooner you can go home." He opened the door and led Morris out into the hall. "Hey, I know the name of a great psychiatrist. Would you like me to write down his number for you?"

Morris shook his head. "I don't think I'll be needing that," he said. "An hour with Hattie is more therapy than I can take."

❖ ❖ ❖

Even with antibacterial soap and a nailbrush, it took Morris several washings to get all the blood and dirt from his arms. The white porcelain sink ran red and brown with the sullied water.

"I hate to bring this up," said the cop overseeing his booking, "but you might want to go to a clinic and get tested sometime soon."

"Tested for what?" Morris asked.

"Well, you have some open cuts," he said, "and a couple of pints of that guy's blood on you. Chances are you're fine, but you never know."

Morris reached for a towel. He suddenly felt weak. *What have I gotten myself into?*

The fingerprinting was a short but smelly process that required another hand washing when it was done. After that came the mug shots. He held the narrow plaque of numbers beneath his chin.

This can't be happening.

The camera flashed. He felt as if he had climbed into a Wild West jail scene for a photo at the amusement park downtown. If only he could figure out how to climb out.

An hour later he emerged from the maze of holding cells a clean but clammy mess and found Hattie waiting patiently in the lobby. *Poor Hattie. What a way to spend a Saturday.* He sidled over to her.

"You poor, dear boy," she said quietly, patting his cheek. "What were you thinking?"

"I wasn't," he replied. "That was the problem."

She led him out of the station to a car hugging the curb.

"Where did you get this?"

"I borrowed it from a friend." She squeezed his arm. "I had some shopping to do and didn't feel like fighting for a seat on the subway. I was in the checkout lane when my phone rang." She shook her head. "The good detective was the last person I expected to hear on the other end."

Stricken, Morris mumbled an apology.

"Let's get out of here," she said. "I'm hungry."

"Hattie, I'm not fit to go anywhere," he protested. "Look at me. There's blood all over my shirt."

She deliberated for a moment, then brightened. "I've got some shirts here in the car." She dug around in a shopping bag in the backseat and produced a fresh black T-shirt. "I bought them for my nephew. He's not quite your size, but this one might fit."

Morris smiled. "You do think of everything, don't you?" He took the offered shirt and stretched the sleeves a bit before putting it on. "Oh, Hattie, I don't know about this." His arms bulged from the sleeves, and his chest strained against the thin cotton.

"Don't be ridiculous," she said, bristling. "This is how all the guys are wearing them now. Besides, we're going to lunch whether you like it or not."

He climbed into the car. "I won't even try to argue with you."

"Good," she chuckled. "Now let's get as far from here as we can."

Far turned out to be his favorite deli several miles from

the school. Most of the vinyl booths were empty, he noted with relief. He was not in the mood for a crowd.

"You sit there," Hattie said, pointing to a booth. "I'll go order our food."

He sat down obediently and waited, picking at his nails. *So that's it? I say I'm sorry and wash my hands and life goes on?* He would have felt better, in a way, if they hadn't let him go. *I broke a man's jaw today. I spilled his blood.*

Hattie reappeared with a tray of food. "You won't believe this," she said, "but the guy behind the counter wouldn't take my money. He said, 'Heroes eat for free.' He recognized you from your picture in the paper."

Morris felt sick. "Did you tell him where we just came from?" he asked wryly.

"Now that you mention it," she said, lifting a forkful of Caesar salad, "what happened this morning?"

He bit into a pickle spear and chewed thoughtfully.

"You are not a violent person, Morris," she continued. "What possessed you to lay into someone like that?"

He sighed. "He was involved in the shooting. One of the other guys said so."

Hattie dropped her fork. "Are you sure?"

"He all but admitted it there on the court. I think he would have if I hadn't . . . interrupted."

"Do the police know?"

"I told them," he said. "They're going to interview a witness, then head over to the hospital to see the guy today."

"Whew." Hattie took a gulp of her iced tea and sank back into the booth. "I am so relieved."

"Yeah, I feel good too," he said, "knowing that justice will be served somehow in the end."

"That's not what I mean." She looked him in the eye and

pointed her fork at his head. "I'm relieved that you don't have a screw loose." She paused. "At least there was a reason for your actions. What you did was wrong, but at least it makes sense."

He shivered and instinctively checked his hands for blood. "I just can't believe I did it. I didn't think I was capable of something like that."

"We're all capable of evil, Morris. Every one of us. It's just human nature."

He opened his mouth to argue, but she cut him off. "Besides, you have a tremendous amount of anger. You need to learn to forgive."

"Forgive?" he sputtered. She said it so matter-of-factly, as if she were telling him to wash his hands or eat more vegetables. "Hattie, do you hear yourself? We're not going to forgive those guys. They tried to kill us. They tried to kill the kids. No one's going to forgive them."

"God will forgive them if they ask," she said quietly, her eyes on the table.

"How do you know that?"

"Because," she said, "He forgave me, and He'll forgive you too."

"And what did we do, Hattie?" He leaned across the table. "What did we do to almighty God that was so horrible that we need to be forgiven?" He felt the sodden weight of Vice's bloody head in his hands and bit his tongue.

"I don't think I need to answer that," she said quietly.

"So what? We screwed up. Haven't we suffered enough? If you ask me," he muttered under his breath, "God doesn't sound all that terrific."

"Morris." She was startled. "Don't forget about Jesus. He—"

"Awww, Hattie," he moaned, "don't throw this Jesus stuff at me. Not right now."

He could feel her squirming beneath her cool veneer, desperate to give him an answer, but she didn't speak. They fell into silence, occupying themselves with their food. He wiped his mouth on a napkin.

"Pardon my asking," he said, "but how much can you know about forgiveness? I mean, from what you've told me, your life thus far has been pretty wonderful."

"Yes," she said, "it has. But I've had some special training in forgiveness."

"What do you mean?" he asked.

A long moment of silence passed before she spoke.

"When I was in college I lived alone for a while," she said. "I had always shared a place with my sister, but I wanted to know what it was like to really be on my own. My mother told me it wasn't a good idea." She sighed. "But you know how stubborn I can be. Anyway, I got my own apartment. It wasn't in the best part of town, but it was all I could afford. I drove my own car, cooked my own food, and had a grand old time." She looked away. "One morning I went to the grocery store. When I came back there was a man in my apartment."

He set his sandwich down. *Please don't let this be what I think it is.*

"He had just robbed a liquor store up the street . . . and to celebrate, he beat me up and raped me."

"Oh, Hattie . . ."

"For months after that I just wanted to die. My family tried to comfort me with platitudes and clichés. My friends at church dragged me to prayer meetings and quoted Bible verses to me. Everyone meant well, but it didn't help." She smiled at him sheepishly. "It just made me madder. The only thing that kept me going was my hatred for that man. I wanted him to suffer. I wanted him to be punished for what he did."

"Did they catch him?" Morris asked.

"No, they never did. But after a while I started to see him, and myself, as God sees us."

He knew he would regret asking, but he couldn't help it. "And how is that?"

She smiled, and he could almost read her mind. "As people who need to be forgiven. That's what we are, after all."

"Hattie." *I don't think I agree with what you're saying.* "I'm so sorry that happened to you. I never knew."

"It's not exactly something that comes up in everyday conversation. I do have a reminder of it with me all the time, though." She stroked a curved scar along the side of her knuckle. "He broke a vase in my apartment, and I cut myself on one of the pieces."

Morris whistled under his breath. "You're a better person than I am," he said. "I'm nowhere near forgiveness, or even manageable anger, for that matter."

"That's okay," she said. "I just hope you get there someday." She wadded her napkin into a ball and tossed it onto her plate. "Now, can I trust you to start acting like a civilized human being? Because if I ever have to pick you up from the police station again, I'll kick your butt from here to next week."

He smiled. "Believe me, my days of random acts of violence are over." He glanced at his watch. "It's already three o'clock. I was supposed to stop by my mom's this afternoon, but I won't have time if I'm going to make dinner for Sheri at six. Maybe I should just cancel."

"For heaven's sake, don't do that," she said. "Spending an evening with Sheri Wallace is the best thing I can think of for you."

"How am I going to explain my . . . unusual appearance?" he asked, touching his face.

"Tell her the truth," Hattie said. "She'll understand."

He felt his lip. "Easier said than done."

"Well, you should have thought of that before you became a one-man wrecking ball."

"Yeah." He carried their trays to the trash. "Yeah, I know. Let's get out of here. I've got a lot to do, and fixing up this ugly mug might take a while."

"Wish I could help."

He gave her a lopsided smile. "Thanks. You've already done too much." He caught her arm. "Thank you." There was nothing else to say.

Chapter 12

Morris stood before his bathroom mirror with a tube of Neosporin in his hand. He dabbed more cream on his lip and practiced a smile. The effect was ghoulish. *Okay, I won't smile.* Maybe if he turned the lights down low enough, she wouldn't notice.

A delicious smell wafted from the kitchen. Candles flamed on the dining room table. Jazz crooned from the radio in the living room. Everything was perfect except his face. He just hoped she would understand. He ran a lint brush over his sweater and headed back to the kitchen.

He cracked the oven door and peeked at the lasagna. Bubbling cheese was always a good sign. He drizzled a fresh vinaigrette over the salad, stopping to pick at a lingering splotch of ink beneath his nail. How long would he bear the stain reserved for thieves and drug dealers? *My criminal days are over.* He turned his attention to the salad. *But what if they're not? What if this isn't over?* He tossed the spinach weakly. Just a few hours ago he beat a man senseless. How did he know he would never do it again? Nothing had changed since he held Vice's limp head in his hands. A shower and a change of clothes hadn't changed what he was. *Have I always been this way?*

He jumped at the knock on the door. Was it six o'clock already? He scanned the room. Everything was in place. He set a bottle of wine on the table and opened the door.

"Hi." Sheri smiled in the doorway.

Something pleasant fluttered around his heart. Was it possible that she was even more beautiful than the last time he saw her? Her hair fell softly over her shoulders. Her skin shone luminescent in the candlelight. Her eyes . . .

"Morris! What happened to you?" A crease puckered between her brows. She touched his jaw lightly and turned his head to get a better look. "Were you in a fight?"

"Actually, I was." He took her coat.

"What happened?"

"First, let me tell you that you look beautiful," he said.

She blushed but didn't look away.

"Why don't we have some dinner, and I'll tell you the whole sordid story."

He pulled out her chair, and she sat down obligingly. Thank goodness he had remembered to slide a book of matches under the short leg of the table. It held steady as he poured her wine and sat down across from her. She waited expectantly.

He passed her the salad. "I went to play basketball this morning the way I do every Saturday."

"With Congo and those other guys?" She had a good memory.

"That's right. Everything was going fine until I overheard

a conversation between Congo . . . and one of the guys involved in the drive-by yesterday."

"No," she gasped.

"Yes." He hesitated. "When I heard what they were discussing, I guess I just snapped." *Is that what happened?* "I . . . uh . . . I was just so angry. That guy could've killed all of us. The kids . . . " *He could have killed you.* Morris hung his head. "I beat him up pretty bad."

"Does he look worse than you?" Sheri asked.

Vice's pummeled face flashed before his eyes, and he nodded. "Yeah. He looks quite a bit worse than I do."

"Oh, Morris." She laid her hand over his. "What's going to happen? Are you in trouble?"

Her hand was warm, and his arm thrilled at the pressure. *I should get into trouble more often.*

"I had to go to the police station, but luckily Detective McCloski was there. He said that if Vice doesn't press charges, I won't be in any trouble."

"Who's Vice?"

"Vice is the . . . well, I guess he's the victim in this situation."

"But he's also the guy who shot our playground to shreds yesterday?" She set her glass down heavily.

"Yep. He's one of the guys. McCloski went over to the hospital this afternoon to arrest him."

"Hospital?" she squeaked. "You put a man in the hospital?"

"I was really angry, Sheri. I had no control. I just . . . I just lost it."

"How are you feeling now?" she asked.

"Honestly, I'm a little scared. I never knew I was capable of hurting someone like that. It's almost enough to make me doubt my sanity."

She picked up his hand. "I probably would've done the

same thing," she said. "You were acting on instinct, like a bear protecting her cubs."

"You would have done the same thing?" he asked incredulously.

"Well, I would have tried. I don't know how much damage I could do to anyone."

He smiled with the left side of his mouth. "I'll tell you what. You can beat me up later. For practice."

She curled her fingers into a fist and laughed. "I might just take you up on that offer."

"I can't wait," he said. "But if you'll excuse me for a moment, I'll get our dinner from the oven first." He loped into the kitchen and returned with his gaze focused on the pan of lasagna in his hands. "Hey, do you think we could forget about what happened earlier today? I'm really not too proud of my escapades."

"All right, then. Let's just forget about it."

"I know it won't be easy, what with my lovely visage and all."

"In a strange way I kind of like it," she said. "It's rugged and manly."

This is why I love you, Sheri. He raised his glass. "You're an angel. Here's to an evening together."

"Here's to enjoying the moment." She smiled and clinked her glass against his.

❖ ❖ ❖

An hour later, Sheri flopped onto the couch with a groan. "That was the best cake I've ever had." She patted her trim waist and sat up. "I hope my stomach isn't bulging out."

Morris laughed. "I don't know if that's possible," he said and scooted imperceptibly closer to her.

"But seriously," she said, "what's in that chocolate sauce you drizzled over the top? I have to know."

"I'm sorry, I can't tell you that. It's a trade secret."

She knuckled him in the ribs. "If I weren't so full, I'd beat you into submission, boy."

"Boy?" he protested. "Girl, you're four months younger than I am, thank you very much."

"I guess that's right." She leaned against him and sighed a full, happy sigh. A saxophone purred from the radio. Trumpets blared in the semidarkness. A candle burned low on the coffee table. "How is it," she asked lazily, "that I know your deepest, darkest secrets, but I never knew you liked jazz?"

He slipped his arm around her shoulder. "I don't know," he answered. "I know your deepest fears, but I wasn't sure if you'd like walnuts in the salad. I suppose it's the same thing."

"I loved the walnuts." She frowned. "Wait a minute. What do you mean, you know my deepest fears? You don't know my deepest fears."

"Sure I do."

"Name one."

"Badgers."

"Badgers?" Her voice jumped an octave.

"Remember the time you found a badger in the dumpster? I thought you were going to die on the spot."

"It screeched at me," she said defensively. "It tried to attack me. Besides," she added, laughing, "who expects to find a badger rummaging through a dumpster in the middle of the city?"

He chuckled, remembering. "I don't know where it came from, but I remember you wanted to catch it and put it in Vern's car."

"I was just trying to pay him back for that awful April

Fools' joke with the glue." She couldn't stop laughing. "I don't know that badgers are my biggest fear, but they're near the top of the list."

He dried his eyes. "I guess we skipped the formalities and jumped straight into the important stuff when we met," he said. Her profile was charming in the candlelight. "Actually, I still remember the first time we met."

"You do?" she asked. "Tell me."

He shifted his weight, and she nestled against him.

"You were wearing a black shirt," he said, "and I remember thinking you looked like the angel of death."

She sat up. "What? You'd better be kidding, Morris."

He dissolved into a pile of helpless laughter as she swatted at him.

"No," he said, swallowing a giggle, "you looked beautiful." Suddenly, he wanted to tell her everything. He couldn't help himself. "You've always been beautiful." He pushed the hair from her face. "Your eyes and your smile . . . you shine. You're like a star."

She reached around to stroke the back of his neck, and he melted at her touch. "I've always thought you were devilishly handsome."

He grimaced. "Emphasis on the devil." He took her hand in his and opened his mouth without thinking. "So, you want to be my girlfriend?" *I can't believe I said that. I've been hanging out with too many third graders.*

"Yes," she blurted and then blushed. "Yes, I do. If you're serious."

He wanted to yell; he wanted to leap off the couch and dance around; but most of all he wanted to kiss her. *How does this work?* They had been friends for so long, perhaps the protocol was different.

"I'd like . . ." he started, then tried again. "Would you . . . may I . . . ?"

"Please," she said.

He grasped her face in his hands and kissed her. Her mouth was softer than he had imagined. His lip throbbed, but pain had never felt so good. She fell against the couch as they pulled apart.

"This is the best date I've had in a very long time," she said.

⁂

They talked late into the night. Morris lit a new candle when the one on the table drowned, crackling in a pool of its own wax, and they talked until the second candle was sputtering.

"I'd better go," she said at last. "It must be two in the morning."

He glanced at his watch. "One forty-five," he said. "That's what I love most about you. Your uncanny ability to guess the time."

She dropped a kiss on his forehead and retrieved her coat from the chair. "Thank you for dinner, dear," she said with a grin.

"It was my pleasure, babe," he replied.

She wrinkled her nose. "Babe?"

He stalled. "Um, sweet pea?"

She shook her head.

"Honey?"

She deliberated for a moment. "Yes," she said, "I can live with honey. Just not in front of the kids." She grinned wickedly.

He rose from the couch and took her hand. "I can honestly say," he declared, "that tonight was one of the best nights of my life."

She squeezed his hand with a faint pressure.

"C'mon," he said. "I'll walk you to your car."

Chapter 13

The receiver trilled twice in his ear before Sheri picked up. "Hello?"

Her voice made the room seem brighter. Outside the window the sky was a deeper blue.

"Hi, beautiful," he said, reveling in the freedom of finally voicing his private thoughts.

"Mor-rr-isss," she drawled, "what an unexpected pleasure."

He wondered what she was doing. Was she sprawled out on the couch watching TV? Grading tests at the kitchen table? Painting her toenails?

"What's my main squeeze doing on this fine Sunday afternoon?"

"Well, right now I'm curled up in my favorite chair by the window." There was a smile in her voice, and he could almost see the dimple in her chin.

"I caught you napping, didn't I?"

"Is it that obvious?" She yawned. "I thought I sounded pretty alert when I answered the phone."

"Let's just say I know you well enough to know what your Sunday afternoons consist of. In fact"—he pinched his forehead and closed his eyes—"I bet you're watching the home decorating channel on TV, snuggled up in that afghan Hattie crocheted for you."

She sighed happily. "Guilty as charged, my dear, guilty as charged. What did you do today? It was really nice out, wasn't it?"

"Yeah, it was sunny and clear all morning. I went over to my mom and William's for brunch when they got home from church."

"Oh, how did that go?"

"I was glad to see them." He hesitated. "Although my mom latched on to me when I tried to leave and almost didn't let go."

"I don't blame her," Sheri said. "I wouldn't let you out of my sight if you were my son. You've been living a strange and dangerous life lately."

"Mmm."

"I don't suppose you mentioned your run-in with the police yesterday?"

His neck tightened in a guilty spasm. "No, I didn't. The last thing my mother needs is another reason to worry about me."

"Didn't they wonder about your face?"

"I think they assumed the scrapes and bruises were left over from Friday's adventure. It was all I could do to steer the conversation toward more cheerful topics." He laughed. "You've never heard so many questions about eggs Benedict."

"You've got a wonderful family, Morris. They really care about you. All of us should be so blessed."

"Yeah, I guess it's nice to know I'm loved."

He closed his eyes and saw his mother's teary smile again. He saw William's outstretched hand and felt the hearty clap on his back as he entered their apartment. It was spotless, as usual. A rumpled dent in the couch, a candle burning on the mantle, and an open book on the coffee table were the only evidence that it was lived in at all. Warm smells drifted from the kitchen.

"Your mother is making her famous eggs Benedict," William had said. "She hasn't made them since our first morning together in this apartment." He handed Morris a glass of orange juice, and they sauntered into the dining room.

"That's beautiful." Morris pointed to an oil painting on the wall behind the table. "Is it new?"

"We picked that up last weekend at an estate sale," William said.

Morris followed the bold slashes of black and blue across the canvas. Fingers of yellow bled in from the opposite corner. "It's . . . unusual," he murmured, tracing the patterns in the air. "Like light piercing the clouds of a gathering storm."

William grunted his understanding as Sandra appeared from the kitchen with a tray of food. Morris couldn't remember the last time he had seen her so happy.

Sheri's voice broke into his thoughts. "You are," she said.

"What?"

"You said it's nice to know that you're loved, and I said you are."

"I'm sorry. My mind wandered for a moment." *Is she telling me she loves me? How do I respond?*

"What were you thinking about?" she asked.

"About a comment William made this morning. He was quoting from the sermon they heard at church, and he said something about 'all have fallen.' I don't remember it exactly, but the gist of it was that everyone falls short of God's standards. Like we're all a bunch of rabid sinners waiting to kill each other." He thought uneasily of the restless mob waiting at the train station each day.

"Wow," she murmured. "That's heavy."

"I don't know," he said. "It just doesn't seem like that can be right."

She sighed into the phone. "Well, a few days ago I would have agreed with you, but after the shooting I'm not so sure."

He chewed at his nail. "But if it's true, shouldn't this God they're talking about have some responsibility toward us?"

"What do you mean?"

"I mean, shouldn't He have some obligation to get us out of the mess we made? We're just the dumb humans. He's the almighty One. He's supposed to be loving."

"Oh, man," she muttered. "I never thought of it that way."

He could sense the crease forming between her brows. "I'm sorry. I'm making you think way too hard for a Sunday afternoon. You should be napping."

"Well, I wouldn't mind getting back to sleep," she said. "I was dreaming of you."

He felt a surge of warmth. What he wouldn't give to be curled up with her in her favorite chair.

"I'll see you tomorrow, beautiful," he said.

"I can't wait."

He hung up the phone, lay back in the chair, and closed his eyes. *What a woman.*

❖ ❖ ❖

Morris shivered and pulled his knees to his chest. It was so cold. Had he left a window open? *That's going to wreak havoc on my electric bill. How long have I been asleep?* He opened his eyes.

A misty moonlight flooded the dark, quiet room. His breath hung frozen in the air, and he thought of the billowing clouds of steam that rose from the factory where his father had worked. The echoes of grinding machines and falling snow and tires scraping against ice fled from his mind. *What have I been dreaming of?*

He shifted uncomfortably in the hard chair. The floor in the kitchen creaked at a footfall, and he held his breath. It came again, more than just the settling of aging wood. It was the sound of shifting weight. He leaped to his feet. The mist fell away, and the moonlight grew brighter as he lifted his head.

"Who's there?" he barked. "Get out of my house." He jumped forward. His forehead met with something solid, and spots danced in his vision. What was going on? He gripped his head and squinted against the radiant moon. *Leaves.* There were leaves. A twig poked into his ear. He was stunned by a blast of cold as he dropped to the ground and dragged himself free of the overarching branches. *Oh, God, I'm sorry.*

He wasn't in his chair or even his apartment. His knees turned to water as he tried to stand. *I didn't know.* He had been curled up on the ground beneath the tree, *the* tree, the only tree that ever really mattered. As he watched, a cold tongue of gleaming white fire snaked around the trunk and through the branches, moving like a wisp of fog over the road on a winter day.

A movement in the branches caught his eye. They dipped beneath the weight of something that wasn't there before. A shudder crept along beneath his skin, pushing his hair up on end as he remembered the woman. Where was she? Was he too late? He turned his head to listen. Not a sound. Nothing stirred. *Maybe they left. Maybe she knew better than to eat the fruit.*

The branches tossed and creaked as the tree spread its

arms and exhaled a loud breath of frigid air. A soft ringing rose with the sighing of the leaves, and he sank to his knees. In the branches, a high voice quivered like a plucked string and broke into beautiful song. He wanted to cry. Behind the song he heard his father laughing as his mother's voice joined in and sang along. *How can anything so beautiful be wrong?* He fell on his face, and the cold, lilting voice pressed him sleepily into the grass.

He opened his eyes and saw two feet on the other side of the tree. The calves tightened as the legs rose up on the toes, and the body leaned into the branches. *This can't be happening.* Leaves fluttered to the ground like falling stars, resting pale and bright in the deep shadows of the grass. He shook off the smothering wail of a song and crawled toward the tree, cutting a wide berth around the burning trunk on his hands and knees before emerging on the other side.

The chiming voice was unbearably loud, and he swayed drowsily under its blare. It pushed all thoughts from his mind but those of the firm, golden fruit clasped tightly in Eve's slender fingers. He dragged his eyes from her hand and peered into the tree. The lizard crouched dark as a bit of night against the shining branches. Its tiny beak was open wide, and he could see down the tunnel of its throat to where its heaving sides pumped out the hypnotic song. Its black eyes rolled back into its head as it wailed through the leaves.

Eve pressed the round, honeyed fruit against her cheek and breathed deeply from its fragrant skin. *No.* He wrung his hands and reached for it as the song droned on. His fingers brushed against her hair, and she turned away. *Just let her eat it.* His chest tightened with longing. He wanted her to take a bite. He wanted to see what would happen and if the rich, shiny orb was as sweet as it looked.

A glad voice crashed through the trees beside them. The man emerged with a smile and an outstretched hand, then stopped short, freezing at the sight of the fruit clutched in her hand. Morris could see that Adam would be no help at all.

"Stop her," Morris pleaded. "Stop."

Adam touched the fruit that touched Eve's face, and she pulled away with an accusing glance. He reached for her with an open palm and spoke a pleading word. She lowered her eyes to the fruit and turned her back to him.

Frantic, Morris scanned the trees for any sign of help. Where was God? Eve looked from the tree to Adam to the fruit, with a furtive glance toward Morris, who caught an animal gleam in her eyes. He sprang forward as she raised the fruit to her lips.

"No!" he cried. Dark juices spurted from the fruit as she plunged her teeth into the golden flesh. She shivered with delight as it dripped down her face, leaving a crimson stain on her chin. She thrust her hand toward the tree, wrenched another fruit from its stem, and gave it to Adam, who looked at her shining face and the sweet red juice dripping from her fingers and took a bite.

The song stopped, the leaves rustled, and the lizard disappeared. The man and the woman turned their backs to one another and munched greedily at their fruit, oblivious to the sudden silence. Morris waited. Where were the fire and brimstone? Where were the pestilence and plague? *Maybe I was wrong. Maybe nothing will change after all.*

He turned back to the tree with a smile starting at his lips, then fell to the grass, stunned to momentary blindness by a searing flash of cold, white fire that shimmered on the trunks of the forest and cast twisted shadows on the ground. The woods blazed around him, bobbing disconnectedly in the pale, clear light, and as he lay prone a biting frost stung his skin and chilled him to his very bones. He writhed and rolled over, searching helplessly for Adam and Eve in the burning, blinding whiteness. In the center of the ravaged tree, a fire burned like the midday sun.

This is it. Morris struggled for a breath. *Judgment Day.* He closed his eyes, and an image grew in the bleary brightness behind his lids. A little boy lay on the ground, huge eyes staring vacantly from his shrunken face. Wrist bones and ribs strained hungrily against his wasted skin, and flies swarmed in a cloud over his body as his eyes rolled back into his skull. His jaw fell open against his sunken chest as he breathed his last.

Morris shot forward, and visions crowded him on every side. A child squealed in pain as his father whipped him with a leather belt. *No!* An old woman crumpled to the ground with a cry. *Please! God!* Soldiers crawled through a seeping field. "I don't want to die," one whimpered, and then a bullet tore through his neck, and he fell with a gurgle into the mud. *Stop!* A car crept around the corner of an icy street. Snow whipped at the windshield and piled around the tires as the driver strained to see the road from inside. He pumped nervously at the brakes, easing the car down a hill. A patch of ice shone faintly in the streetlight as the tires crawled onto the slick, whipping the car into a spin. The driver cranked frantically at the wheel, to no avail, and houses flew toward him, picking up speed. He barreled down the hill, and with a horrifying jolt the car leaped a curb and smashed into a telephone pole, the trusted seat belt tearing helplessly to the side. He shot through the windshield and flopped limply onto the hood, head dangling from his broken neck. Clouds parted above him, revealing the winter stars. So beautiful . . . so quiet.

"Oh, God!" Morris screamed. "Make it stop!"

In a burst of light he rushed back to the garden, where Eve was eyeing Adam with a critical gaze. Her eyes traveled the length of his body, crossed the ground, and moved up the length of her own. She began to tremble and cried out in dismay, ripping at handfuls of leaves and flinging them across her body. Adam dropped his fruit, scrambling for the shelter of the trees. He yanked frantically at a vine and barked an accusation her way. She sank, weeping, to the ground and covered herself with her hands.

Suddenly they froze. Morris felt it too: a Presence drawing near. *Oh, God! I tried to stop them.* He crawled back to the shelter of the burning tree. Eve dragged herself beneath a bush. Adam darted from his hiding place to kick the cores of the eaten fruit under a tree. *It's too late. He already knows.*

The Force advanced upon them. The woods bowed as in a great wind and fell silent. Eve wept softly with one hand clamped over her mouth, while the other hid her eyes from view. Tears streamed through her knuckles and fell hot upon the grass. Adam plastered himself against the rough bark of the tree. His eyes jumped from the sky to the heap of clumsily buried fruit to Eve and back to the sky as his mouth crumpled in a frightened sob. Morris felt a prodding gaze sweep over them and hid his face. *Oh, God.* He saw in his mind the searching eyes, the burning, branding, watching eyes that saw them snuffling in the dirt. Why were they hiding? *He knows.*

Adam jumped to his feet and stripped a branch from the tree where he cowered. He clutched it to his chest and stammered a high-pitched reply to a question Morris didn't hear. *Is he conversing with God?* Morris peeked from between his elbows and saw Adam babbling to the empty clearing in a flustered sweat of shame. Morris felt another question posed in the still, Eden air, as two bright spots flamed in Adam's cheeks. He spat a word like poison from his mouth and pointed to where Eve lay. She crawled, facedown, into the clearing and sobbed a reply.

The air thundered with an unheard command, and the impish lizard dropped from its hiding place in a nearby tree, frothing at the mouth and gnashing its tiny jaws as it slunk into the clearing. Its eyes bulged painfully, and it bristled under the piercing gaze of the Presence. A pronouncement was made. The sprightly creature writhed in pain as its limbs withered before their eyes. It shrieked as if it had been bitten, then shuffled out of sight on its suddenly swollen stomach.

The Presence turned its gaze to the man and woman, huddled in the slick horror of shame, and Morris felt it watching him too. His skin crawled with a clammy regret. *I didn't stop them. I didn't want them to stop.* His lips stung with the bitter flavor of the fruit he longed to taste. *Look away.* He felt the eyes upon him, his soul laid bare in the clearing, and willed his trembling legs to run. He cleared the tree by a few steps before he pitched forward. Streaks of light danced before his eyes. He wobbled to his feet and ran on.

The tempting tree, the clearing, and the cowering couple faded behind him, but the Presence pursued him still. He felt it blowing at his back closer than the wind. *I can't outrun Him.* It darted before him and blocked his path. *God help me.* He turned to the side and ran. His legs were failing; he couldn't breathe. *I'm ruined.* A cliff jutted into the sky at his left. He ran, and still the Presence followed. *I'd rather die.* He sprinted to the crumbling edge of the gaping ravine. *I'd rather die.* A rush of wind overtook him as the punishing Presence closed in. He wondered if he would see his father in death and jumped.

Chapter 14

Morris walked into the school and stopped in surprise. A few yards away, Hattie was heaving a huge sigh and marching through the waiting arms of . . . a metal detector? A buzzer squawked and a line of plastic lights flashed above her head.

"Oh, for Pete's sake," she muttered. "You'd think there was a metal plate in my head." She dumped her keys and loose change into a tray offered by one of the uniformed guards and smiled sweetly. "Let's give it one more try, shall we?"

Morris scratched his head. "Hattie," he said. "What's going on?"

She glanced at him over her shoulder. "This is my fourth trip through this contraption." She tapped one of the silent posts with her fingernail and marched through again. "I keep setting it off for some reason." On the other side she emerged with her fingers in her ears. The buzzer was silent. "Whew. I thought you'd have to frisk me for a minute there." She laughed.

The guard flinched but didn't smile.

Hattie grabbed her keys. "Keep the change," she said.

"No," Morris called after her. "I meant, why are there metal detectors at the entrance of the school?" He looked the guards over. "The kids aren't going to bring guns in here. The guns are out there." He stabbed a finger toward the doors.

A uniformed woman rolled her eyes as if he were a child, took his arm, and led him through the machine. "Watch your head," she barked.

He ducked.

"Violence is a problem for schools all over the country," she said. "We're just trying to protect you."

Morris felt the heat climb into his face. "The problem is out there," he repeated. "We need guards patrolling the playground, not watching the doors."

Hattie grabbed his elbow and steered him down the hall. "Don't pick a fight with the security people, Morris," she said. "It's only Monday, and I'm too tired to rescue you."

He followed her, stealing a glance over his shoulder as they walked away. As one of the guards bent to pick up something from the floor, a studded black grip poked casually from beneath his jacket.

"They have guns?" Morris hissed. "This is ridiculous."

Hattie nodded. "It is. It's quite possibly the worst idea in the history of humankind."

In his mind he saw Eve sucking hungrily at her stained fingertips. *Not the worst.*

Hattie continued, "Talk to Vern. I'm sure this is one of the school board's brilliant ideas." She laughed. "At least you only had to walk through it once. Those guards have no sense of humor. I think that one guy thought I was coming on to him." She disappeared around the corner.

A cheery whistle floated down the hall from the cafeteria, and Morris spun on his heels and headed the other way. *I'm sorry, Vern. I just can't deal with you right now.* Actually, he didn't want to run into anyone, not Vern or Hattie or Pete or even Sheri. *Where can a guy just get a little peace and quiet?*

The answer was clear. He grabbed a bucket of cleaning supplies and a pair of rubber gloves from the closet and headed to the boys' bathroom, where the dim corridor of empty stalls gleamed like the Promised Land.

He began scouring the dingy sinks until his forearms ached. The spotted mirrors came next and then the gritty tile floor. By the time he reached the urinals, his fingers throbbed and his back ached, but he didn't want to stop. His mind was blessedly occupied. When the door swung open, he looked up with a sigh. Even the kids who couldn't read should recognize the yellow "Closed for Cleaning" sign. He squinted at the figure, backlit by the brighter lights of the hallway. The face was a blur, but the boots were unmistakable.

"Those little boys don't exactly have the best aim, do they?" Vern said.

Morris dropped the brush and rose stiffly to his feet. "Forgive me if I don't shake your hand."

Vern chuckled and shook his head. "Hattie told me you were a mite upset by our new security measures."

Morris turned away.

"They were the only way the school board would let classes continue as scheduled." Vern ran his hand through his thinning hair. "They would've closed the school for days or even weeks if we hadn't agreed to the metal detectors."

"I know. It's not your fault," Morris sighed. "But those

metal detectors and guards are ridiculous. We're put through airport security while potential shooters are out roaming the playground. And why do they have to carry guns? We don't know who these people are. Do we really trust them enough to let them roam the school with weapons?"

"We don't have a choice," Vern answered. "No one ever said the school board was bright, Morris. They're just in charge."

"That's comforting. I guess might makes right after all."

"Morris, we do what we can."

"I know." He forced a tight-lipped smile. "Thanks for keeping the school open."

Vern laughed. "Heck. I'd be so bored if they closed the school, I think I'd lose my mind."

Morris turned his attention to his work and hoped Vern would take it as a signal to leave.

"Well, I'd better get back to work. I've got a school to run. I'll . . . uh . . . I'll see you later."

Morris waved without looking up. The door eased shut. He chucked the toilet brush at the far wall and lowered himself to the floor. He couldn't believe he had been so rude to Vern. What was wrong with him? *I can't stand to be around anyone today. I just want to be left alone.* He laid his head against his knees and closed his eyes.

Okay, God. I get it. I'm wrong. I'm suffering. Enough already. But he knew it wasn't enough. It would never be enough. Blood tinted the shattered glass and the snow in piles of rosy red along the street. Vapor stretched in a thin line from the smashed radiator into the dark, winter sky, and a wisp of a dying breath puffed through Saul's cold lips as he lay broken on the hood. *It'll never be enough. Someone has to pay for what we did.*

Suddenly his head swam. The checkered tiles of the bathroom floor swung back and forth before his eyes. He could hardly breathe. His stomach rolled over and clenched, and he grabbed the bucket just in time. He coughed but nothing came. His ribs clapped together, and he heaved again, but still his mouth was dry. Open bottles of disinfectant littered the floor. *Must be the fumes. I need a drink.*

He left the supplies where they lay and staggered out the door, wiping the spittle from his mouth with the sleeve of his shirt. A grim-faced guard stood with his spine pressed against the wall at the entrance to the cafeteria. Morris averted his eyes and slid past him. He strode carefully to the pop machine and fumbled with a handful of change. Why was he so nervous? Was the guard watching him? *Don't look at me.* He snatched his Coke and jogged out the doors and toward the art hall.

Where am I going? I've got work to do. He pushed the thought from his mind and kept moving. He glowered at the guard posted outside the music room as he passed. *What do they think we're going to do? Do they blame us somehow for the shooting? Do they blame me?*

He jogged around a corner and stopped. One small corner of the art hall lay deserted before him. The doors of the busy classrooms were closed. He sank against the wall with a sigh. A row of pencil drawings lined the opposite wall—an army of grim little faces and vacant eyes. They sent a shiver up his back. *What's wrong with these kids? Aren't any of them happy?* He turned to leave, more depressed, if possible, than before, when a blur of color in one drawing caught his eye.

The crooked, gap-toothed grin was disproportionately large and filled most of Sophie's round head. She had apparently scribbled a dark cloud around the page to signify her hair and spent the rest of the class coloring an elaborate pattern of rainbow colors over her clothes. *A spot of sunshine in a dreary world.* But what was that in the background? Just outside her black expanse of hair stood a smiling, waving, brown-bearded figure of a man. *Of course. It's Jesus.* Morris pressed his hands flat against the wall, breathed deeply the clean scent of the pencils and the paper, and felt better. Of all the people he knew, Sophie was the only one he cared to see that day. *Maybe I'll find her at recess.*

He pushed himself back from the wall and squared his wide shoulders for the unpleasant task ahead of him, namely, finding Vern and apologizing. He was developing quite a knack for apologies. He headed back to the bathroom to finish what he had started.

The morning slid past in a fog. When he found Vern, the principal waved off his apology as if the hurt were no more than a fly circling his lunch and offered Morris a bratwurst.

"It's elk," he cackled and watched Morris chew the wild meat. "My brother shot this tasty critter a few weeks ago, had it made into sausage, and sent me twenty pounds of the stuff." He eyed the link dubiously. "I think I'll throw a party for the teachers one of these weekends. A barbecue, to be specific."

❖ ❖ ❖

According to the school board mandate, recess was held in the gym with a security guard posted at each entrance. The teachers rolled their eyes at one another and whispered behind their hands but smiled politely at the guards as they passed by.

"What's up with the rent-a-cops?" Morris heard one teacher whisper to her friend.

"Maybe if they put these guys outside, we'd be able to use the playground," the other replied. She plugged her ears as a shriek bounced off the wall. "I feel like a firecracker in a tin can."

When Morris stopped by again toward the end of the hour, the guards were rubbing their temples and digging in their pockets for aspirin. *Oh, come on. You can fight off armed intruders and defuse bombs, but you can't take an hour with a bunch of noisy kids?*

After work, Morris took his lunch and found a solitary bench at the park. A thick layer of pearly gray clouds dimmed the afternoon sky and trapped the budding summer heat near the earth, and the air was unusually still. He caught glimpses of the city's bustling business district from where he sat: corners of buildings and banks of shiny windows and flashes of yellow as taxis zipped through the streets. Sirens droned from somewhere nearby, and he wondered what was going on. A warehouse fire? A heart attack? A robbery?

⁂

He was vacuuming the teachers' lounge the next morning when Sheri stumbled through the door and wove unsteadily across the room. She collapsed on the couch, and he sank down at once beside her.

"Whoa, are you okay?" She shook her head, and he smoothed her hair away from her face. "Sheri, what's wrong?" His heart throbbed painfully in his chest. "Are you hurt?"

She whispered something he didn't hear.

"What?"

"Sophie was shot yesterday afternoon," she sobbed.

Sophie? "She . . . what? Shot? By what?" The strength drained from his body.

"By a gun, Morris." She wiped her nose on the back of her

hand. "There was a shooting. Some kind of gang thing, and she got in the way."

His arms went limp. "Oh." Visions of doctors huddled around the little girl and tubes and white beds and beeping machines filled his mind. *Poor Ken. I wonder if he's waiting at the hospital alone. I should go over there.* He cleared his throat. "What hospital did they take her to?"

"Morris," Sheri choked. "Morris, she's dead." She turned her face into the back of the sofa and bawled.

"She's not dead." He patted her shoulder.

"What?" She sat up on a shaky elbow. "Morris, she's dead! They shot her right through the heart."

"No, no. She's not dead," he said soothingly. "God loved her." It was a sick mistake. "He might not care for the rest of us, but He loved Sophie." There were lots of little Asian girls in the city. "He wouldn't let that happen to her." He wouldn't kill off one of His own.

"She's dead," Sheri wailed.

Morris scooped her into his arms and held her against his chest like a frightened child. "Shhhh." He traced circles on her back. "She's not dead." His head throbbed and his eyes burned. Tears ran down his face and soaked into Sheri's mass of curly hair. *She's not dead.* He squeezed her against his chest. "She's not dead," he sobbed. "He wouldn't. Not Sophie." *Oh, God.*

Sheri tried to pull away, but he held her tighter. "Shhhh." He thumped her back. "She's not dead."

The room caved in on him like the crumbling walls of a tunnel. He heard Sheri calling him, but she was so far away. *She's not dead . . . not dead.*

Chapter 15

Morris jerked open the small drawer on the left side of his dresser and plunged his hand into the mess of silky snakes, searching for a narrow length of black. *Does it smell like my father's funeral?* He held the tie to his face and hoped for a stale reminder of the pain, the lilies, and the smell of crushing sorrow in the cold mortuary air. *Did my mother's tears bleach the color from the front?* He looped it under his collar and knotted it as tightly as breath would allow, then left without looking in the mirror.

The sky was dappled with shining clouds that bleached from gray to white as they sped across the sun. Morris buttoned his coat against the breeze, turned the corner, and started toward the massive stone church ten blocks away. Across the street a woman pushed a stroller into the wind, mindless of her sleeping child until they jostled over a crack in the sidewalk, and he let out a wail. A girl on a skateboard zipped past them and launched herself into the line of cars that crawled the street. Horns blared and fingers waved. Thumping stereos rattled the windows of glitzy sports cars. An eager couple pawed at each other in the back of a passing taxi. Life went on.

They don't know any better. The thought ached unbearably. *They don't know that she's gone.*

Several blocks later he stopped at a flower market for a spray of white buds on a thin, brown branch.

The vendor eyed him curiously. "Is this all you want, son?"

Morris nodded.

"Are you all right?" the peddler asked, handing back his change.

Morris nodded and squeezed a stubborn tear back into his eye.

The tall iron steeple of Ken's church poked into the sky just a block away, grasping vainly at the clouds and causing Morris to falter. The tear burst from his eye and landed on his lip, and his legs wobbled beneath him. The air grew thicker with each step, and buildings around him began to sway. *I can't breathe.* He stumbled onto the steps of the church and collapsed, buried his face in the crook of his elbow, and wept.

He closed his eyes and saw the blunted bullet boring a path through Sophie's thin frame. Did it hurt? Did she suffer, or was she blessed with the rising numbness of a quick death that caught her unaware?

A warm hand squeezed his arm. "I miss her too." Hattie sat down beside him and took his hand in hers.

"I can't do this. I can't. She's not dead . . . not until I see her there," he snuffled. "Until I walk into that church and see her . . . coffin . . . there's still a chance that this is all a mistake. That Sophie's still alive, off playing somewhere in the sun."

Hattie handed him a Kleenex. "Honey," she whispered, "Sophie is dead."

He sopped the tears from his eyes and blew his nose before he looked at her.

"She's gone from this world but happy in another. You know that, don't you?" she asked quietly.

Morris shook his head. "No. Honestly, I don't. I can't believe that a God who would end a life like hers is any good at all."

"But, honey," Hattie said, "she's with Him. She's happier than we can begin to imagine."

He thought of Sophie's drawing hanging on his refrigerator and wondered if her smiling face would join the Asian woman and the bearded figure on the hill.

"How do we know that?" he asked weakly. "How do we know that God isn't making her pay for our mistakes? That seems to be the way it works." He felt himself building steam. "We screwed up, and now we're paying for it. No hope of reprieve . . ."

"Morris," she interrupted quietly, "that's *not* the way it works."

The bell in the church tower clanged three notes to call the last few mourners through the doors, and he helped her up. As they passed through the entry, an unholy sadness pressed him into the floor. He followed Hattie blindly through the halls toward the sanctuary, catching glimpses of color and light as they went. Sunlight spilled across a poster of smiling children with Bibles in their laps, while a cheery nursery glowed in bright pastels.

Morris cringed at the memory of the starving child and the gaping throat, the lash of the father's whip and the bleeding boy. A large painting of Jesus, bearded and beatific in His fluttering robes, graced the hall ahead. Morris searched his pockets, sick at the crowd of beaming children flocking to the Savior's embrace. If only he had a pen, he would crack open the gilded frame and sketch a bloodied Sophie with a bullet in her chest on the ground behind their precious Jesus. *Then they'd see how much He cares.*

"Morris," Hattie called in a low voice. "Let's go, dear."

He straightened his jacket with a sigh and followed her into the sanctuary, his eyes trained on her broad linen back. He would have preferred to sit farther back but kept his mouth shut and squeezed as close to the end of the pew as he could as they shuffled into the second row.

Despite the mass of dark suits and dresses, the room reveled in the bursting glory of spring. Bits of stained glass worked into the wide windows along each wall cast a rosy glow, while soft white sunlight poured over the carpet. Birds twittered happily outside. Creamy lilies propped in vases at the front of the church and tied in clusters at the end of each pew made the scene entirely too cheerful. *More like a wedding than a funeral.* It had the same restful spirit as the library and seemed like the kind of place he would have liked to spend time in on any other day.

A body appeared next to him at the end of the row.

"Hi," Sheri whispered.

He made room for her beside him and tucked her hand under his arm. How did she manage to be so beautiful with such puffy eyes?

"I can't believe how many people are here."

The rows across the aisle were packed with squirming kids and their equally uncomfortable parents. He recognized only a few of them from the school. The rest must have been families from the church. Whispered questions broke the silence.

"Why did Sophie die?"

"Am I going to die too?"

"Is she in heaven?"

The parents shushed their children, straightening their ties and smoothing their unruly hair with practiced hands. Behind the families, Sophie's teachers circulated Kleenex, dabbing their eyes and longing for a cigarette to mourn with. Vern was perched in the middle of them. He caught Morris's eye and nodded solemnly, for once without a smile. Morris didn't recognize the rest of the faces, but they seemed strangely familiar. Sorrow had settled heavily around their mouths and dulled their eyes until they all looked the same, like figures carved in stone. *Is that what I look like?*

Pete Goreman squeezed into the end of their row. "Mind if I join you guys?"

"Of course not." Morris leaned over to shake his hand.

Sheri snuggled closer to him to accommodate Pete, and Morris was glad. She was warm and sweet and living beside him; he couldn't get her close enough.

Morris stiffened. Six men in dark suits were coming down the aisle, bearing Sophie's coffin. He had known when he walked through the doors of the church that it would be waiting inside, but nonetheless the horror of that tiny wooden box was stifling. *Oh, God . . .* He was going to be sick. Sophie's cold, lifeless body was wreathed in flowers and stuffed into that shiny box, soon to be dropped into a gaping pit dug specially for the purpose of giving her a quiet place to rot. He gulped loudly, and Sheri squeezed his arm.

"Are you okay?" she whispered, but he didn't respond.

Ken Ling appeared at the back of the sanctuary and walked steadily up the center aisle. Morris couldn't see his face, but he seemed to be concentrating on every step. He reached the front of the room and turned slowly, as if an arthritic joint made the movement painful, to address the crowd. He began to speak, but Morris couldn't make out the words. A low-pitched sob rose in his memory, and soon the mournful wail was all that he could hear. He closed his eyes.

❖ ❖ ❖

A drenched handkerchief moistened Sandra's hand, unable to absorb another tear as Morris, willing his knees to obey, led her down the aisle of the small church to the row reserved for family. He jerked with a stab of remorse at his father's initials embroidered in the corner of the cloth. Tears threatened his eyes, but he bit them back, gnawing on his lips until they bled. Crying would only make him look guilty.

Saul's friends from the paper mill filled most of the available seats, and extra chairs had to be placed in the back for their neighbors and other friends. Morris lifted his eyes to survey the host of sorrowful faces. *My father was a good man.* He fixed his eyes on the wilting white roses strewn across the box and tried not to think about what lay inside. *Fourteen.* There were fourteen roses with long, light stems. *No thorns.* The petals were browning at the edges. The coffin and his mother and the church softly bled to nothing around one white flower lifted higher than the rest. He imagined the rose blooming in a fresh green field. It swayed in a summer breeze and lifted its bobbing face to the sun.

His mother squeezed his hand until his fingers ground together. "Morris, let's say good-bye to your father." As they slid from their seats, the crowd of mourners filed in behind them in a line that stretched out the back of the church. The coffin loomed large before them. *Look at the flowers. The flowers.* His mother leaned over the dying box until the petals touched her face. He held his breath.

"I love you, Saul," she whispered fiercely, then collapsed over the coffin in a storm of tears. "Oh, Saul," she sobbed and wrapped her thin arms around the box as if she were wrapping them around the man inside. "My Saul."

Oh, God. She's touching it. He felt faint. The smell of the roses was suffocating. *I'm sorry, Daddy.*

❖ ❖ ❖

Hattie stirred beside him. He blinked and turned in time to see her beg pardon and climb discreetly over the others in their row until she gained the aisle. At the front of the church she stood beside Ken, and together their tears trickled over their cheeks and down their arms to their clasped hands. Ken cleared his throat with an effort.

"I've asked Miss Hattie Graeble to say a few words." He faltered. "To . . . uh . . . share her memories of Sophie. When she's finished, please feel free to come forward and share your thoughts as well."

Hattie dabbed at her eyes for a moment, then tucked a tissue resignedly in her pocket. Morris could almost read her thoughts. *What does it matter? We're here to mourn, aren't we?*

"Sophie Ling wasn't even in my class," she started, "but she was one of my favorite students."

His mind wandered as she spoke, and he saw Sophie beside him on the playground bench in her yellow jacket. *"Who is this?" he heard himself say. "That's my mom," she answered softly. "She died when I was three."*

Sophie melted into memory, and the sanctuary reappeared. *What's with this family? Are they cursed?*

". . . And strange as it may sound, this precious child's death should cause us not to mourn but to rejoice," Hattie blubbered, "because she's at home with the Lord where we long to be."

Morris balled his hand into a fist at his side as Hattie twisted a cheap plastic ring from her finger and laid it on the coffin with a sob. "Thank you," she whispered and made her way back to her seat.

Already the line was forming. One person after another babbled tearful platitudes about God and heaven while Morris gnawed at the end of his tongue. They looked like a pack of yelping dogs fawning back to the master who whipped them.

Fools. The more you love Him, the worse it will be for you. He looked at Ken's shaking hands and wet face. How could he bear it? To lose both his wife and his daughter at the hands of the God he served?

The line wound down, and people took their seats. The coffin was covered in mementos: trinkets from the children and drawings and bouquets of flowers left by grieving hands. *C'mon, people, she can't take it with her.*

He watched Ken's flooded eyes trace the ceiling in search of a sign from heaven. None came, and he lowered his head in what Morris imagined was defeat. *There must be a spark of anger somewhere behind that deluge of tears.* He rested a hand on the coffin and squared his shoulders. *This is it.* Morris leaned forward with his chin in his hands. *Somebody's finally going to hold God responsible for this.*

"I'd like to share a few final thoughts with you before we proceed to"—Ken's voice dropped to a whisper—"to the cemetery."

Are you listening, almighty God? Your people are about to figure out what's what.

"My Sophie's death is a tragedy." He patted the coffin. "Perhaps one of the greatest losses the world will ever know.

But we must remember," he continued, lifting his head, "that God isn't blind to our pain."

Morris snapped to attention.

"He knows what we're feeling. He also lost a child when He gave His Son to pay the debt of our sin."

Hattie "mmm-mmed" at his side, and quiet voices "amen-ed" and "hallelujah-ed" behind him. He couldn't believe it. Had they lost their minds? He wanted to yell. He wanted to knock the coffin over and drag Sophie's limp little body before them and poke his finger into the bullet hole in her chest. *This is your God!* he wanted to scream. *This is how much He cares.* He leaped from his seat and bolted up the aisle, away from the coffin and toward the exit.

A bustling figure followed him. "Morris," Hattie hissed. "Young man, get back here."

He ignored her and burned through the halls, past the nursery, past the missionary table. He stopped at the drawing of Jesus with the children and worked a wad of saliva into his mouth. He cursed the picture and spit on the floor.

"Morris!" Hattie was close behind, but he sprinted out the doors.

A small knot of reporters waited hungrily outside.

"Sir! Can I ask you a few questions?" A camera hovered in his face.

"Was the funeral well attended?"

He groped for the first collar he could find and pushed. Its owner tripped and rolled backwards down the short set of stairs.

"Morris!" Hattie was steaming.

Why don't you go whine to God, and maybe He'll knock me off too? He quickened his pace, but he heard her steps crowd together in a burst of speed. Then he felt her full weight unexpectedly on his back, and they crumpled together to the cement.

"Do I have to knock you down to get your attention?" she yelled. "Would you walk out on Sophie's funeral? Would you dishonor the memory of our little friend like that? You might as well go spit in Ken's face." She stopped to catch her breath, and when she spoke again her voice was low. "You might not agree with what he believes . . ."

"Agree?" he snarled. "Not only do I not agree, I think you've all lost your minds. God doesn't love you. He sure didn't love Sophie."

Hattie opened her mouth.

"No!" he shouted. "I don't want to hear it. Your precious God is still punishing us for something that happened a long time ago. And He's not even punishing the right people. How all-knowing can He be? He killed my father." *I killed my father.* "He killed Sophie. Who knows who's next? It could be you. There's no forgiveness; there's no mercy."

Hattie grabbed his arm and pulled him around to face her. Her breath was hot on his neck.

"Are you deaf or just stupid? Didn't you hear what Ken just said? Let me make it easy for you: 'For God so loved the world that He gave His one and only Son, that whoever believes in Him shall not perish, but have eternal life.' "

"What is that?"

"It's a verse," she said, "from the Bible. Would you like another? 'This is love: not that we loved God, but that He loved us and sent His Son as an atoning sacrifice for our sins.' "

Enough already. He stepped back and put up his hands in surrender. "I'm sorry, Hattie. I can't believe that."

Tears clustered at the corners of her eyes. "Why wouldn't you want to believe that?"

He shook his head. "I can't believe in a love like that," he choked. "Not for me."

"Why not?" she pleaded.

His father's mangled body hovered before his eyes. "I just can't," he whispered and turned to walk away.

Chapter 16

"Owwwww." The scruffy young man moaned as a pair of rough hands pushed his face into the wall. His dark hair straggled in greasy wisps over the collar of his battered denim jacket. He looked as though he hadn't eaten in a day or two and hadn't bathed for considerably longer. "I don't know, man," he whined. "I told you I don't know nuthin' about that." His eyes flickered in nervous circles. "I swear I don't."

A shadowed face bent close to his. "I know who your friends are, Tony, and I know what they're into." One hand held Tony fast while the other produced a slip of paper. "This is my number. Call me when you know something."

Tony wriggled loose and backed, wide-eyed, away from his assailant.

"I know where to find you," the voice said. "Don't forget it."

Tony turned and fled from the alley into the light and relative safety of the city street.

A moment later Morris emerged from the shadows, shaking slightly. He spit into a trash can, but the taste of his words still lingered. What had he become? A ruffian? A thug? *More like an enforcer.* He rubbed his jaw. *Someone has to pay.*

He forced himself to relax and felt his face slip out of the angry set it had held for days. He was tired. It didn't matter if Tony didn't know who killed Sophie. Someone did, and he was going to find that person.

Across the street, Morris could see a pair of cops drinking coffee from Styrofoam cups on the steps of the police station. He couldn't believe it. *What are you doing? You've got a murder to solve.* He started across to give them a piece of his mind but, remembering the stale stink of the holding cells, veered off to the sidewalk. The police, of course, were conducting a formal investigation of the shooting, but Vern had told him it wasn't going so well.

"According to McCloski, they're having trouble finding witnesses," he said. "You know how tight these neighborhoods are, especially when it comes to gangs. I guess no one wants to talk."

But someone had seen what happened. Morris took a right at the police station and headed south along the street away from Quiley Heights and into a rougher neighborhood. *Someone is going to talk.* His stomach grumbled, but he didn't want to waste time looking for lunch, as it was already early Friday afternoon. Vern had suggested he take a few days off of work to pull himself together, and Morris had gladly agreed, but despite keeping his ear to the street for the past two days, he had no leads on Sophie's killers. He was no detective, but even he knew that the longer a case went unsolved, the colder the trail became.

The cracks in the sidewalk widened to chasms as he walked. The streets were pitted and potholed and buckling, and litter rolled along in the gutters pushed by a breeze that smelled heavily of fast food. He was entering the forgotten alleys of the city's ghetto, where no one cared enough to pick up the trash, and the mayor never promised to repair the crumbling roads.

He loped past a pile of sagging tenements. Children screamed from inside, and radios blared. A woman draped herself over a fire escape in the sun. She laughed as he walked past and raised a suspiciously fat cigarette to her lips. She took a lengthy drag and laughed again.

"You want some, baby?" she called after him weakly. "Good stuff."

Morris jogged to the next block, where a tiny shack of a restaurant jutted from between the brick buildings. It seemed to be constructed of old boards someone found in a dump and nailed together in a rough square. A plump tabby prowled through the door and rubbed against his leg, its green eyes split by velvety black slits. A vision of frolicking tigers flashed through his mind, and he felt a stab of longing near his heart. A toothless old man grinned at him from the doorway. *Maybe they've heard something in there.* He paused at the door and coughed as the stench of burning oil pushed over him in a cloud. *Nah. They probably don't even speak English.*

A car stereo thumped from somewhere up the street. Experience told him that expensive stereos in poor neighborhoods meant gang members, drug dealers, or the underlings associated with them. *Just the kind of guys I'm looking for.* He followed the vibrations in his breastbone up another block and around the corner to a street of grubby matchbox houses on tiny plots of dirt where the grass refused to grow. Railroad tracks sprawled at the end of the street in a testimony to urban decay, and Morris could only imagine how little the residents slept with a train thundering past every hour of the night.

He turned his attention to three tough-looking characters gathered around a car in front of a crumbling bungalow. One of them languished in the driver's seat with the pounding radio, where Morris guessed by the open hood and scattered tools all the money had gone, while the others batted each other playfully in circles. Morris recognized the one in the car as one of Congo's friends.

"C'mon now. I'll teach you good." One of the circling thugs laughed and cuffed the other's ear.

"Oh, you want to fight? I'll fight." His friend put up his hands and threw a couple mock jabs into the air. His bulging biceps were a canvas of mottled tattoos, and Morris could only make out a few of the gruesome designs.

"Shut up. You're makin' my head hurt," the one behind the wheel griped. The others stopped cavorting and looked up as Morris approached.

"What d'ya want, man?" asked the tattooed one.

"I want to know," he said quietly.

"What? Speak up, man."

"I want to know," he yelled over the jolting music, "who shot the little girl on Monday."

The music stopped, and a face poked out of the driver's window. The two outside the car started to complain.

"Shut up!" their friend said. He turned to Morris. "You're the guy from the courts. You almost killed Vice."

What can I say? I'm sorry? I'm not. "Yeah, that was me."

"What do you want?" He looked almost frightened, and Morris felt a brief twinge of pity.

"I want to know who killed the little girl."

The one fighting off his tattooed friend swore loudly but turned his back as the driver shot him a look.

"What little girl? You're talkin' crazy." He forced a laugh between his teeth.

"The little Chinese girl. On Monday. I know it was an accident," he added.

There was a scraping sound from beneath the car as a figure emerged in the gravel. Congo set down the wrench he had been using, then looked at Morris and picked it up again. He swallowed heavily and licked his lips.

"Hey, man, what's goin' on?" he asked casually, getting to his feet. "I haven't seen you since—"

Morris took a step closer. "Who did it, Congo? I know you know."

Congo backed away. "I don't know. I swear to you I don't know." His eyebrows peaked helplessly in his forehead, and his body sagged until the wrench fell with a clang to the ground.

Morris wasn't convinced. "Yes, you do," he said. "You know something, and you're going to tell me."

"No—no," Congo stammered.

His friends muttered threats from behind him.

"Who do you think you are?"

"We could take this punk."

"Get out of here!" Morris yelled. They skittered away. "Now"—he leaned his chin into Congo's forehead—"I know you know someone who saw what happened. You know my number, and I know where you live. Call me."

Sweat ran in rivulets between Congo's eyes. He nodded without a word and backed away.

"Call me," Morris repeated and strode out of the neighborhood as quickly as he could without arousing suspicion. No one flat-out ran in that part of town unless he had just stolen something or killed someone. Morris felt sick. He hated acting like that. *Then why do it?* The thought annoyed him like a mosquito mining at a naked patch of skin. *Someone has to pay. God's too busy getting even with the rest of the world to deal with whoever killed Sophie.*

"He gave His one and only Son . . ." Hattie's voice rang in his memory. Maybe God could love some people. *Maybe taking Sophie isn't God's way of punishing her but of punishing me.* The thought made him want to wretch.

"I took a life," he mumbled. *It was an accident.* " . . . A life was taken from me." *It's my fault.* A crack in the sidewalk grabbed his shoe, and he tumbled onto the pavement. He rolled stiffly to his feet and rubbed his stinging palms. Maybe there was love for some but not for him. He reached the bustling city street and turned toward home. *Not for me.*

He pitched his keys at the kitchen counter as he dragged himself through the door. They skittered across the Formica and landed on the floor with an abbreviated jingle. He looked around. Sticky dishes filled the sink and spilled over onto the counter. Pizza boxes were stacked on the dining room table, shoes and T-shirts littered the living room, and the air smelled stale. The light flashed on his answering machine.

"Hi, Morris. It's Sheri."

As if I wouldn't recognize her voice. Does she think I'm forgetful or just crazy?

"I hope you don't mind me calling. Hattie and I are really worried about you. She . . . um . . . she said she saw you yelling at some homeless guy on the street yesterday."

There was a pause, and he could feel her fidgeting.

"Anyway, we'd love it if you'd call one of us and let us know how you're doing. I . . . we love you, Morris. Don't forget that. Bye."

He deleted the message without listening to it again. He'd

call them later, when the whole mess was resolved. They'd be so proud of him, cracking a case even the police couldn't solve, bringing Sophie's killers to justice. Maybe it would erase some of his guilt. *Maybe.*

There was a timid knock at the door. He crossed the room in two strides and fixed his eye to the peephole, flinching at the sight of his mother and William waiting outside. They huddled together on his welcome mat, their longing faces pinched by the glass eye. Sandra had been crying. *The last thing I need.* He held his breath and waited until their muffled voices filtered through the door.

"I guess he's not home," William said.

"He hasn't been home for days," his mother moaned.

William stretched his arm across her shoulders and gave her a gentle squeeze.

"Don't worry, Sandra. Morris is a sensible young man. He's not going to do anything foolish. Let's go home. We'll call him later." He steered her around, and they started down the hall.

I'm such a jerk.

Nevertheless, it was a relief to see them go. He stretched out on the couch and waited for the phone to ring. Darkness would fall in a few short hours. Night would creep into the city, and uneasy tattlers would release a collective breath of relief as thugs tucked into the mindless sleep of theft, rape, and murder that characterized their evenings. Someone would call soon to tell him in the anonymous shadows of the night what couldn't be said under the watching eyes of the afternoon sun. He cracked his knuckles and wondered what he would do to Sophie's killers. There were so many possibilities. He closed his eyes and tried not to think about stray bullets and tearing flesh.

Chapter 17

Morris twitched to life from a shallow sleep. Was that the phone? How long had it been ringing? He groped blindly for the receiver but felt instead the warmth of human flesh. *What is this?* A forest of shinbones and thickly calloused feet hemmed him in on every side. He loosened his grip on an ankle and sat up, only to knock his head against a knee draped in rough cloth.

A crowd of men pressed in on him, oblivious to the waking body at their feet. Their foreign tongues wagged without pattern, spraying Morris with spittle in their excitement. He rolled onto his elbows and wriggled his way through the herd of hairy calves and stamping feet. A cry erupted from the mob, and money exchanged hands as the men cheered and groaned in turn, old cronies watching a game at the corner bar.

He broke free of the crowd, rolling into a pile of sand, and staggered to his feet. *Who are these guys?* They looked like the waiters in his favorite Middle Eastern restaurant. *What are they doing, and why is it so dark?* Clouds puckered over a sunless sky in a preternatural twilight, but the ground still radiated a dry midday heat. Swarms of black flies danced over the men like tiny shadows come to life. The wind tossed a handful of dirt against his back.

I don't remember Eden being so dry. Through the shadows he saw dusty hills in the distance, dappled by groves of trees and vineyards oozing sweetly in the heat. Craggy foothills rose against the clouds far away. Another gust of dirt stung his face and wormed into his watering eyes. He didn't need to be told that he wasn't in paradise anymore.

Softer voices babbled behind him, and he turned from the men with relief to a pair of barefoot women huddled together in the blowing sand, their eyes fixed on something behind him. The younger of the two gripped her friend's arm in a sudden spasm and began to wail. Her thoughts played out before his eyes.

"Whore!" She was thrown to the ground on a rocky hillside. Feet kicked as she fell, catching her ribs until she cried for mercy. Handfuls of sand pelted her eyes. She wiped the spit from her face with shaking hands and thought about death. Would it hurt? Would her accusers be merciful? Make it quick? She dared not lift her face to the swarm of sneering men, but she knew that there was no mercy in them. In a last, desperate glance she searched the hills behind them for the help that she knew wouldn't come.

They picked up rocks and weighed them thoughtfully in their hands. In the end it didn't matter. Any rock would do. She covered her face as they pulled their arms back and took aim at her skull.

"Stop!" a voice rang out. Arms hesitated and fell. Who dared to interrupt them? Their business was official. It was their right, and justice had to be served.

A young man pushed through the mob. Her heart leaped within her chest. Was He the One? The One who put flesh on withered legs and light into eyes long blind? Who defied the religious rulers and dined with the tax collectors? But what would He think of her? Didn't He know what she was? What was He doing?

Then one by one the crowd departed, muttering angrily. Rocks clattered to the ground at her feet. She felt a hand on her shoulder and knew they were gone.

"Go," He said, and she trembled at His touch. He spoke with such authority. "Go, daughter, and sin no more."

Morris felt the warmth of His hand, the jubilant throb of her heart, and knew that in one moment her life had changed. She looked past Morris and took up her mourning with a husky sob.

Suddenly, the blood fled from their cheeks, leaving their faces pale beneath their tanned skin. Morris felt sick. He had seen that look before. A few months ago an unfortunate bicyclist met with a bus outside his apartment. No one in the tearful huddle of bystanders wanted to look at the grisly explosion of metal and skin, but none of them could look away.

What are they looking at? Another woman, slightly older, joined the mourners with a sob that sparked a spasm in his chest. *Do I really want to know?* He turned around and stepped back a few paces, craning his neck. *Oh, Jesus!* His stomach turned.

The figure appeared one piece at a time as he stepped away from the hill. First, the bloodied face, a mash of cuts and bruises. The left eye was sealed in a pouch of blackened skin, the right eye no more than a slit in the swollen face. Gashes ringed the forehead, and blood seeped over the brow. The cheeks flamed in a fiery rash where the beard had been torn out, and only scraggly tufts of hair remained. Another step, and the mangled torso hovered above him. Flesh was torn to shreds along the rib cage, exposing bits of gleaming bone. The body hung tacked to wooden cross beams by impossibly swollen wrists. Another step, and Morris stood even with the women. From there, he could see the legs and the blunt iron spike nailed through the feet. *Jesus Christ!* He doubled over and wretched into the sand.

As if in answer to his call, the man turned His head. Something rattled in His throat as He took a labored breath.

Oh, God . . . Was it true? The Son of God on a cross? What was it Hattie said? God sent His Son as a sacrifice for sin? In a flash he saw it all: the starving children, the dying faces and pestilence and plague, the armies marching off to war, the bullets bouncing off the playground, Sophie's startled cry as her heart split in two, Vice's skull cracking in his hands, his father's car spinning out of control . . . and all the time the dying body of God in human form dangled before him.

He clawed at his eyes. *Stop it. I don't want to see any more.*

The women wailed behind him and beat at their chests.

Why is this happening?

Jesus rolled His one good eye toward Morris. "Someone has to pay," He wheezed.

⁂

Morris woke with a yell. His skin was crawling. He checked himself for blood. *What is that?* The phone chirped in his ear.

"Hello?" he yelled. His hands shook.

"I know who killed the little girl," said a muffled voice.

"Who is this?"

"I know who killed her."

"Where do you want to meet?" he asked.

The voice named a place in the neighborhood Morris had visited that afternoon.

"I'll be there in an hour."

Chapter 18

Morris stepped into the street at half past nine. The streetlights surrounding his building had burned out long ago, and for once he was thankful for the concealing drape of shadows. He felt like the counterpart to a comic book hero, crusading for justice and triumphing over evil in the forgotten corners of the city. He only hoped he would be able to burst forth with enough bristling wrath when the moment called for it.

Faced with the possibility of knowing once and for all who killed Sophie, he felt strangely deflated. The manhunt would soon be over, but she would still be dead. Nothing would change that, and his bright spot of happiness would never shine again. *What am I going to do to her killers anyway?*

He could tell the police. Detective McCloski would surely be impressed. He imagined himself sitting in the courtroom when the verdict was read, watching the faceless forms of Sophie's killers shuffling away in handcuffs and orange suits to spend the rest of their lives locked in some dank cell, but the prospect wasn't as satisfying as he'd hoped.

Could he take the ultimate revenge? A month ago, he would have sworn he didn't have it in him, but suddenly he wasn't so sure. Mauled faces paraded before his eyes: Pete, Vice, Jesus. In the last couple weeks he had become something he never thought he was. He looked at his hands in the darkness and heard the preacher's voice in his ears: "We are all sinners!" He hadn't eaten the fruit in the garden, but he had wanted to, and he knew he would have, given the chance. He had proven himself to be a violent, hateful, self-serving creature . . . would he become a murderer too?

He turned down a deserted street littered with weedy lots and boarded-over buildings. Silence slunk beside him in the shadows, and he was grateful for a reprieve from the thumps and throbs of the restless city. Behind him a cricket scraped its legs together in the grass. He picked a rock from the gutter with his toe and kicked it along in front of him. *What would Ken say about all of this? What would Hattie say?*

He knew what they would say, and it was almost enough to make him turn around, but he pressed on. He had started this mess, and he was going to finish it. The rock wobbled on its pointed ends, and he couldn't help but think of stained young women and rabid mobs.

An unfamiliar car slid past him on the street, slowing for a moment as it passed, and he shivered despite the pressing warmth of the evening air. *When is it going to be me?* When would a gun poke through the window of a passing car to spit a bullet his way? *I've made enough enemies lately.*

He had never considered the possibility that he might die. He knew it was inevitable eventually, but he had always envisioned himself dying at a ripe old age, snuggled under a quilt and surrounded by generations of children and grandchildren. He never thought about what would happen afterwards, after he sighed his last contented breath and sealed his eyes against the light of day.

He clutched at a chain-link fence to steady himself. Would he come face-to-face with that gruesome apparition? Was that what hell was like? An eternity of wailing at the feet of the bleeding Savior? Of viewing the tortured deaths of your loved ones again and again? Of hearing the sickening crack of his father's neck and his last whimpered cries?

A cab sputtered past in a billow of blue smoke that set him hacking. *Is it too late? Am I doomed?* He knew there was forgiveness for some. Hattie forgave her attacker, and he was sure Ken would eventually forgive his daughter's killers, but how did one get into that club? There couldn't be forgiveness for everyone, could there? Everything he knew of God was difficult, and that was just too easy. Hattie was mistaken. God didn't come to earth to die for a world of sinners. It didn't make any sense. Love like that wasn't real. *Not in this world.*

He gripped his head between his hands and squeezed until his temples ached and he felt reasonably quiet again. He had to keep going, if for no other reason than to satisfy his morbid curiosity. The assigned meeting place, the back of an abandoned drugstore, leered at him in the glow of a streetlight fifty yards away. He walked on, feeling increasingly nervous with every step.

What am I afraid of? It was a stupid question. *I'm afraid of dying.* Some unsought intuition blared an alarm in his chest. The tornado was headed his way, the nuclear bomb had been dropped, the fire was consuming the building and he was trapped beneath a bureau on the top floor. He fought for control as he darted back and forth from one side of the street to the other, searching the shadows on his way to the store. There was nothing and no one to be afraid of. *Nothing is wrong.* He flattened his lower back against the wall and leaned forward to rest his hands on his knees. *Get a grip.*

There was nothing left to do but wait, and as the minutes passed, his mind crowded with unwelcome thoughts. He wondered what his mother was doing. *Worrying about me, no doubt.* He wondered how she had made it, how she had survived the grief of Saul's death. "The Lord gives and the Lord takes away" was her mantra for the first year following the accident. Although Morris smiled for her whenever she said it, he thought it was the worst excuse he had ever heard. Would she say the same if he were to die?

A trash can rattled in the shadows to his left.

"Who's there?" he barked. Panic distilled to adrenaline, and he balled his fists for a beating. The shadows were silent. A quiet moment passed, then another. *It's just a cat.*

He lowered his fists and looked at his watch. *Is this some kind of joke? Maybe it's a sign.* Maybe he just wasn't supposed to be there. *I'll give him another minute.* He barely finished the thought before a figure materialized beside him.

Morris flinched, startled by the unexpected movement, and wondered how long the fidgety young man had been watching from the shadows. He was small, a full foot shorter than Morris, and sucking shakily on a cigarette.

"What can you tell me?" Morris asked.

The contact took a lengthy drag and looked around. He mumbled something in the same flat voice Morris had heard over the phone.

Morris took a step closer and bent his ear toward the young man's mouth. "What?"

"I . . . uh . . . I'm not sure I can tell you anything." Any hope of sounding intelligent slipped from his speech with the lazy slurring of his words.

"What do you want?" Morris asked. *Don't say money, because I don't have any.*

"Nothin', man," he muttered, turning to the side. "I don't want nothin'."

Morris felt his hands closing into fists again. *Why is he stalling?* "Do you know who killed the girl or not?" he yelled, and the sound of his own voice scared him.

The contact looked relieved. He flicked his cigarette into the darkness and gave a slight nod toward the shadows on his right.

"No, man." His smile revealed a polished gold tooth. "I don't know nothin'."

Another shape stepped forward from the shadows and then another. Morris was surrounded. He recognized a few of their faces from the basketball courts, but the rest were unfamiliar.

"What is this?" he asked.

"Shut up, fool!" one of the faces spat. The others grunted their approval, and in the harsh yellow of the streetlight, the planes of their foreheads and twisted faces hardly looked human.

Morris put up his hands. "I don't know who you're looking for, but—"

"We're lookin' for you," the voice shrilled. "You almost killed our boy Vice. Now you're gonna pay."

Morris sighed. He wasn't in the mood for a fight. *At least McCloski can't bust me for self-defense.*

The owner of the voice stepped into the circle of light, his stiff arm appearing first and his fingers curled around the grip of a handgun. Morris froze. *They wouldn't shoot me.* He glanced around, looking for a sympathetic face in the crowd, a police car, a witness of any kind, but found no help in sight. His heart banged a mayday against his ribs.

The gun bearer turned his arm until the gun lay on its side and raised it to the level of Morris's chest. "Now," he repeated, "you're gonna pay."

Morris jumped back into a wall of flesh. There was nowhere to go and no one to help. Hattie's words rang in his ears: "For God so loved the world . . . " *I'm sorry, Mom.* There was no time. *Jesus!* The finger groped for the trigger. *Help me.*

A brief spark lit the barrel before a weight slugged him numb on his right side. He crashed to the pavement and heard his assailants scatter like frightened roaches at the flicking of a light. *Am I dying?* He felt no pain, but a crushing weight settled over his chest. *How long until I die?* Blood soaked his clothes and dripped onto the pavement. He groaned. *What's wrong with my voice?* It sounded so far away. He groaned again. *That isn't me.* He groped in the darkness at the weight upon his chest until he felt an arm. Someone had fallen on top of him.

No wonder I can't breathe. Can't I even die in peace? He rolled the body onto the pavement and knew in an instant that he wasn't dying. He hadn't even been hit. But which one of Vice's friends had been stupid enough to get in the way? He rolled the body into the light. "Hattie?"

The sight of Hattie Graeble sprawled in an ever-widening pool of her own blood was so unexpected, so ridiculous, that for a moment Morris couldn't move. "Hattie!" he yelled and dived on top of her.

Her neck was cold as he groped for a pulse. "Help me!" he screamed in the hope that someone, anyone would hear. "Help me! Help me!" An erratic pulse flickered against his fingers. Blood bubbled from a dark well in her side.

"Someone help!" he screamed. A car screeched to a halt beside them. *Thank God.* It was the police.

"Put her in the back," the officer barked as he jumped from the car.

"Shouldn't we call an ambulance?" Morris asked.

"In this city? She'll never make it if we wait that long. We need to get her to a hospital. Is she breathing?"

"I don't know." He wiped his slick hands on his pants and bent to lift Hattie into the car. "But she has a pulse." *Oh, God. There's so much blood. Please, Jesus, don't let her die.*

He laid her across the seat and squeezed in beside her, propping her head on his lap as the car sped into the street. His last encounter with the blood-soaked backseat of a police cruiser rose fresh in his mind. *If it weren't for me, none of this would be happening.* He brushed away the rush of blinding tears with the back of his hand.

"What were you doing, Hattie?" he cried. "What were you doing there?"

Her eyelids fluttered at the sound of his voice, and he steeled his heart against the rising hope that she might live. "Hattie," he whispered urgently, "open your eyes. Look at me."

"I've been . . . following you . . . for days. Had to keep you from doing anything stupid." She gurgled what he guessed was a chuckle and closed her eyes. "Happy to take a bullet for you."

It was too much. The dam burst, and the hope of a love that reached beyond reason rushed down to rip the supports out from under him. He fell against the window and wept. "Why?" he sobbed. "Why would you die for me?"

He lifted her up, and in a moment of clarity she fixed her eyes on him. Blood spilled over his hands. "Because," she whispered, "Jesus did the same."

Chapter 19

"Mr. Jackson."

Morris felt a prodding at his shoulder and batted the hand away. It was the first good hour of sleep he had experienced in weeks, curled awkwardly into a hospital chair, of all places.

The hand insisted. "Mr. Jackson."

No. I don't want to know. I don't want to know what happened. He squinted at the doctor through a fog of white walls and floors but couldn't find an answer in the carefully planned expression. Pain gripped his neck and lower back as he straightened in the chair, but he hardly noticed.

"Is she . . . is she . . . ?" He couldn't bring himself to say the word.

"Hattie is going to be fine." The doctor grinned, his professionalism melting in the warmth of his obvious pleasure. "She just came out of surgery."

Morris slumped back into the chair, wrung dry of every drop of strength. *Thank you.*

"It was a miracle she survived." The doctor shook his head. "The bullet missed all of her vital organs and her spinal cord by millimeters. It lodged safely in the tissue of her back where we could remove it without too much trouble."

"May I see her?" Morris asked.

"She hasn't come out of the anesthesia yet," the doctor said. "I'll let you know when you can go in."

Morris rested his elbows on his knees and his forehead in his hands. *Thank You, God.*

". . . He was wounded and crushed for our sins." The smooth voice of the preacher at his mother's church rang in his memory. "He was beaten that we might have peace. He was whipped, and we were healed!" A knot climbed in his throat. *Could it be true?*

He remembered a lunch with Hattie several months ago. "All of us have strayed away like sheep," she told him. "We left God's paths to follow our own. Yet the Lord laid on Him the guilt and sins of us all."

He had brushed her off at the time. *What if it's true?* The last month of his life paraded before his eyes like a witness sent to testify: the garden and the beast, the beating and the shooting and the needle and the blood and the coffins, and hanging over all was the figure on the cross. "Someone had to pay," he whispered.

It was strange, he thought, how the truth revealed itself to him so slowly. It fell from heaven, one shining flake at a time, until he was buried, helpless against the avalanche and packed in on every side by the hope of knowing what was real.

I . . . I believe . . . I think.

The doctor appeared. Morris bounded from the chair.

"Where?" he asked, and the doctor steered him down the hall.

Morris pushed the door open an inch at a time and stepped into the room where Hattie lay. The curtains were drawn across the windows to quiet the morning light. Wheeled machines marked the silence with measured beeps. Hattie lay on her side propped by pillows, her eyes closed, and he wondered if the doctor had let him in too soon. "Hattie," he whispered.

She opened her eyes and smiled at him through a film of sleep. "I can't believe you, boy. After all the trouble you've caused me, you still have the nerve to show up here and disturb my sleep."

"Awww, come on, Hattie, you know you love me." It was so good to hear her voice, he didn't know whether to laugh or cry.

She motioned for him to come closer. "Like the child I never had," she said. "Come here and let me look at you."

He crouched at the side of her bed, and she took his hand. "Are you all right, Morris?"

"Yes," he whispered. "I'm finally okay."

"Finally?"

"I . . . uh . . . I'm ready." The joy was suddenly too much to bear. He wanted to sing. He wanted to tear back the curtains, open the windows, and leap from the building into the sunshine.

"Ready for what?" she asked. "And what's with the grin?"

"I'm ready to believe." He gripped her hand. "Hattie, I do believe."

She dropped his hand, and for a moment he wondered if he should call the doctor.

"I thought you couldn't believe in a love like that."

He grinned sheepishly. "I thought you were delusional. I

thought it was ridiculous that someone would die for me. I thought love like that didn't exist." He bit his lip. "Until you leaped between me and a bullet in a dark alley in a bad part of town."

"Is that all it took?" Hattie chuckled. "Well, I would've gotten myself shot a long time ago if I had known."

A knock sounded at the door, and Ken Ling poked his head into the room, a bunch of tulips in his hand.

"Ken." She beamed. "I'm so glad you're here. Morris, could you give us a moment alone?"

"Of course." He stepped into the hall and began to pace between the vending machine and the water fountain. Seeing Ken stung like the tearing of a newly formed scab. He missed Sophie. He wanted to talk with her, to hear her laugh. Tears welled up in his eyes. *Get a grip, Morris. You know, for such a tough guy you cry an awful lot.*

The door to Hattie's room opened, and Ken stepped out. Morris wanted to run. *What must he think of me?*

"Hi, Morris." Ken stuck out his hand.

Morris shook it and didn't know what to say. "How did you know about Hattie?" he asked.

"One of the nurses on this floor sings in the choir at church. She gave me a call last night."

"Ken, I'm sorry," Morris blurted. "I'm so sorry I ran out of Sophie's funeral. I was just so angry."

"I know," Ken said quietly. "Believe me, I know." He wiped a tear from his eye. "This will be the first Sunday since Sophie was born that I'll preach without her there."

Morris pictured the empty pew where Sophie should have been and felt sick. "What can I do?" he asked.

Ken brightened at the question, and Morris saw the familiar gleam of his daughter in his eyes.

"Come with me. From what Hattie tells me, you could use a good sermon."

"I'll be there," Morris said with a smile. "Just let me make a phone call first."

Chapter 20

Morris fidgeted on the sidewalk outside of the church. He dug his toe into the soil where the velvety pansies bloomed and picked thoughtfully at a hangnail. What if they passed an offering plate? He searched his pockets for cash. He didn't want to be unprepared. It had been so long, so long since he'd darkened the door of a church.

But everything is different now. Everything has changed. His heart swelled with the bursting joy of a thousand blazing suns. His mother would be so pleased. He made a mental note to call her after the service and gave a little hop from one foot to the other. *I feel like a kid again.*

Something clicked inside of him. *Maybe this is what all those preachers mean when they talk about being "born again."* His heart leaped with joy. *I've been given another chance. I'm a new creature. Clean in God's eyes.*

In the distance a vision appeared, swaying closer with

each step. She stepped into the shade, standing beside him beneath the stone archway as he caught his breath.

"Morris, you're glowing," Sheri laughed. "But why did you want me to meet you here? I thought this church was the last place you'd want to be."

He smiled and brushed the hair from her eyes. Children laughed from inside with unconstrained joy. Voices began to sing, and he knew, at last, what they were feeling. An image of Sophie flashed through his mind, leaping into the open arms of the bearded figure in her drawing. *She's home at last. Where I long to be.*

"Morris?" Sheri touched his face, her eyes caught somewhere between wonder and concern.

"Have I got a story to tell you . . ." He saw Jesus stretching out a hand to Sophie, offering an invitation. "There's someone I want you to meet."

"Great." She smiled. "Is he inside?"

"Actually, He's right here with us, right now."

Sheri stepped back and looked him over. "Are you okay?"

"C'mon." He took her hand. "Let's go inside, and I'll tell you all about it."

She shrugged and slipped her hand into his, and he thought his heart might burst with joy. Eden danced before his eyes. *Someday I'll be back.*

SINCE 1894, Moody Publishers has been dedicated to equip and motivate people to advance the cause of Christ by publishing evangelical Christian literature and other media for all ages, around the world. Because we are a ministry of the Moody Bible Institute of Chicago, a portion of the proceeds from the sale of this book go to train the next generation of Christian leaders.

If we may serve you in any way in your spiritual journey toward understanding Christ and the Christian life, please contact us at www.moodypublishers.com.

"All Scripture is God-breathed and is useful for teaching, rebuking, correcting and training in righteousness, so that the man of God may be thoroughly equipped for every good work."

—*2 TIMOTHY 3:16, 17*

The Second Thief

ISBN: 0-8024-1707-8

Meet Tom Ledger. Disillusioned. Bored. In search of comfort and ease. Willing to sell his soul—or at least his employer's most closely guarded secret—to the highest bidder.

Tom has no way of knowing that within hours of committing his first felony, he'll be catapulted into a high-stakes drama as the airplane he's on drops like a rock into a Nebraska cornfield. But as he faces what could be the final moments of his life, even his pitiful attempt at prayer is self-serving: "Please God, please let me live."

The Brother's Keeper

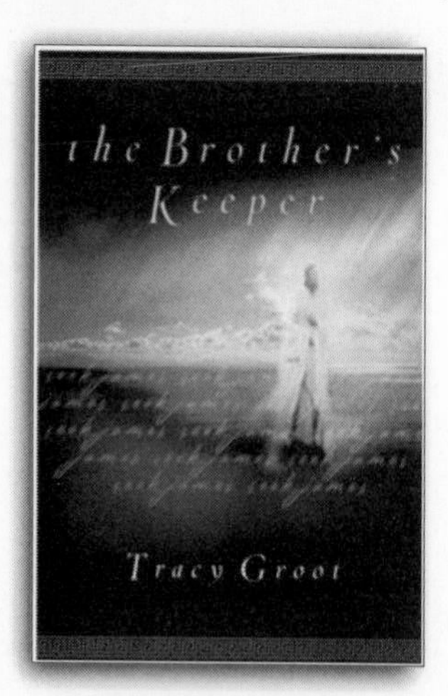

ISBN: 0-8024-3105-4

Thirty years after he followed a star to Bethlehem, one of the Magi is back on another mission. This time, he is sent not to an infant "king of the Jews," but to the king's brother James.

The sons of Joseph run a successful carpentry business in Nazareth. At least, it was successful until the oldest brother, Jesus, left home to tell the world He will forgive their sins and save their souls. Now everyone is hearing outlandish reports of healings and exorcisms. Business is suffering; not many people want a stool made by the family of the local crazy man.

Valkyries Book 1
some through the fire

ISBN 0-8024-1513-X

Streetwise freshman Tracey Jacamuzzi knows that if anyone discovers the whole truth about her, they'll give up on her entirely. She isn't so sure they'd be wrong.

This is where Tracey's story begins—but certainly not where it ends. Because God has set His sights on this young woman. And His plan is to use all of her experiences to draw her to Himself. Along the way, He enlists the help of some unlikely friends.

Valkyries Book 2
all through the blood

ISBN 0-8024-1514-8

Most days, life seems more like a prison than an adventure to Tracey Jacumuzzi. She feels more like a failure than a Valkyrie. And it's no wonder. Her junior year is marred by her parent's divorce, the death of a classmate, and the continued violence of a fellow basketball player.

Tracey's faith in Christ is growing, and she is achieving excellence as an athlete. But she can't seem to control her own actions or rise above her violent past. Even at her lowest point, she begins to understand the potent mercy of the God who refuses to give up on her.

MOODY
PUBLISHERS
THE NAME YOU CAN TRUST.
1-800-678-6928 www.MoodyPublishers.com

THE FALL TEAM

ACQUIRING EDITOR:
Michele Straubel

COPY EDITOR:
LB Norton

BACK COVER COPY:
Julie-Allyson Ieron, Joy Media

COVER DESIGN:
Barb Fisher, LeVan Fisher Design

INTERIOR DESIGN:
Ragont Design

PRINTING AND BINDING:
Dickinson Press Inc.

The typeface for the text of this book is
RotisSerif